Praise for Stuart Kaminsky and his Inspector Rostnikov Mysteries

"Shades of Raymond Chandler and Dashiell Hammett! If you think Stuart Kaminsky doesn't have a feeling for the *best* of both authors, you are in for a surprise."

San Diego Union

"Rostnikov is an exceptionally humane man and a man of many facets. He converses knowledgeably about Gogol, Pushkin and Tolstoy, is a champion weightlifter and enjoys reading Ed McBain's 87th Precinct novels."

Chicago Tribune

"Stuart Kaminsky's novels about Russian Inspector Porfiry Petrovich Rostnikov have been among his finest works."

The Orlando Sentinel

"Stuart Kaminsky has created a sympathetic and engaging hero who solves mysteries in spite of the peculiar handicaps imposed by the police bureaucracy and exacerbated by KGB interference. . . . The Russian setting is convincingly portrayed."

The Cincinnati Post

Also by Stuart M. Kaminsky
Published by Ivy Books:

Inspector Porfiry Rostnikov Mysteries

A FINE RED RAIN

DEATH OF A DISSIDENT

BLACK KNIGHT IN RED SQUARE

A COLD, RED SUNRISE

RED CHAMELEON

An Inspector Porfiry Rostnikov Mystery

Stuart M. Kaminsky

IVY BOOKS • NEW YORK

An Ivy Book
Published by Ballantine Books

ISBN 0-8041-0465-4

This edition published by arrangement with Charles Scribner's Sons, an Imprint of Macmillan Publishing Company

Printed in Canada

First Ballantine Books Edition: November 1989

For
Lucy Irene Kaminsky

The world's full of indescribable crimes—and the criminals are never punished. They continue to rule life and all you do is cry Oh! and Ah!

—Stepan Danilovich Lukin
in Maxim Gorky's *Barbarians*

ONE

A BLANKET OF AUGUST MOSCOW HEAT LAY LIKE A WET cat on Sofiya Savitskaya, burning her eyes as she tried to read by the light of the single bulb in the tiny living room. The window was open, but it brought no breeze, only shrill voices of boys arguing on Balaklava Prospekt two floors below. Her brother Lev's voice was the most piercing, but Kostya Shevchenko's was louder and more demanding.

Sofiya didn't want to listen to them, and she didn't want to read her dark brown shorthand book; nor did she want to go to sleep or go for a walk. There was nothing she wanted to do, but what she wanted to do least was sit in that smothering dark room where she knew before she looked up that the walls of the living room were expanding. She clutched the sides of her chair, trying to hold on, trying not to cry out for help that wouldn't come. This had been happening to her, this room expansion that made her lose contact with life, since she was a child, and she had never mentioned it to anyone. It had always passed, but the terror had grown no less with the years. Once she had tried to consider that the room was not getting larger, that she was growing smaller, but that terrified her even more and became part of the horror. Not only did Sofiya have to hold on to herself during the spells; she also had to fight off the thought that she was getting smaller. If the room was growing, then anyone who walked into it would be in her predicament, but if she was shrinking to become an ant, a roach, her father or brother might walk and step on her.

Once she had tried to scream and discovered that it was impossible when this feeling came, so she had learned to suffer it through alone. Each time she came out of the spell, she was shaken but proud of having made it and told no one, but first the room had to become so enormous that the echo of the thought of her scream would be nothing. She dug her fingers into the dark-wood arms of the chair for the final burst, hearing the voices of her brother and his friends clearly.

"So what can police do? You're just a kid. You say you hit him with your fist, not a rock, stupid."

"Don't call me stupid or it's you'll get the rock, Kostya."

"I wasn't calling you stupid, but I am not afraid to call you stupid. Don't threaten, Ivan, or I'll give—"

Sofiya opened her eyes wide and closed them with an enormous effort as the room snapped back to its normal size, leaving her weak and proud and aware of the promise of a terrible night of fear, heat, and the smell of her father and brother.

She wanted to get up and move to the window, call down to her brother to come up before he got in a fight, not because she feared for him but because she did not want to make the effort to be a part of what would follow. Sofiya couldn't rise. Smeared hands of summer heat and dust pushed beads of sweat trickling down under her print dress between her breasts and thighs, into the hair between her legs, making her shudder and whimper. She closed her eyes once again and opened them to hear her father, who stood before her.

There was contempt in his eyes as he looked down at her, as if he knew her thoughts and feelings, as if he probed her mind and body and shame. Sofiya had seen him look at people this way since she was a small child, but it had always seemed more critical, more direct, when he looked at her and acted as if he knew her guilt.

"I'm takin' a bath," he said, his heavy purple robe on his thin shoulders, a thin copy of *Izvestia* clutched in his stick of a hand. Abraham Savitskaya's body and face were sagging, gray and thin, skin furrowed and arid, his beard, once black, flecked with gray, which matched his skin. Sofiya looked at her father and saw decay and knew no bath would return the moisture and sinew to the man. As much as she had hated and feared his moods in the past, she would have preferred them to this walking death that entombed both the old man and her. Her memory of hatred flared unbidden, and Abraham's gray eyes saw that hatred and glistened with the possibility of long-gone battle. She thought he might strike her for her present thoughts and all her thoughts and feelings in the future. She tensed and awaited the blow, willed it, wanted it, would take anything to make the dry stick of a man who was her father live again in the present, raise her from her chair to battle him and be abused by him, anything to challenge a lifetime of growing smaller in that room with its Moscow-white walls peeling like dead skin.

But the passion had gone from Abraham's eyes before it had even built to certainty, and he turned, went into the hall, and padded to the communal bathroom.

Outside, Lev and Kostya's voices were shout to shout, their faces nose to nose. There would soon be blows, and she would have to pull herself to the window, shouting and hoping a passing man or woman or Comrade Myagou on the first floor would go out and yell at them that the ghost of Lenin would send a bolt of white lightning into the middle of the street as a warning to the nasal children of Israel to swallow their anger and bite their tongues. Sofiya laughed hysterically, imagining the fire of Lenin burning on Balaklava and the old women on their stoops holding their sagging breasts in awe at the ghost stepping in to stop a fight between two boys. At what point, Sofiya wondered, did her father's god step in the way Comrade Myagou promised that Lenin's ghost would appear? Did it take murder, war, earthquake, to stir him to act, or was there nothing in the filth of human conduct that interested him any longer? She imagined God like her father, tired and old and indifferent, which put everything on her thin shoulders, exactly where everything had been since her brother Leonid had died more than a year ago.

Abraham stopped near the bathroom at the sound of her laugh down the hall.

"What?" he shouted with distaste, unwilling to come fully out of his own thoughts and dreams and deal with hers but unable to ignore that single, unprovoked shock of a laugh.

"Nothing," she said, stepping into the hall. "I was thinking of something Maya told me this morning."

Abraham turned his eyes from her toward the open window in search of some Maya of the distant past and then went into the bathroom, locking the door behind him. Sofiya heard him turn on the water and knew he would soak for hours in the tepid water, further shriveling his dry skin, turning him more into a mummified version of that man she could barely remember. She returned to their two-room apartment and closed the door.

Now the voices of the street were screeches and threats and words with no thought or meaning, only the mad offspring of wet heat and boredom as Sofiya pushed herself from the chair, her back soaked with sweat and her bare lower legs sticky. The wooden floorboards creaked when she slowly crossed the room and went to lean out the window into the near darkness. She had to raise her voice over the mad, steady rush of bath water behind and the clash of voices below.

"Lev," she cried, "it's time to come up."

The older boy, whose face was inches away from her brother's, took the call as his sign of victory, and he snickered, triggering Lev, who pushed the bigger boy down three concrete steps toward the basement apartment. The bigger boy's hands went out to grab something, and Lev reached out his hand to help, but it was too late. Kostya Shevchenko's head thudded in the darkness below, and Sofiya called on something in her to respond, but nothing came.

"You all right, Kostya?" shouted Lev in fear.

Kostya came up the stairs, holding his bleeding head and shouting, "Go home to your gimp sister and crazy capitalist father, back stabber." Then he raced down the street.

A trio of boys ran after him, and Lev darted into the building and hurried up the stairs with impossible energy in the heat. The wooden stairs sighed wearily under him and relaxed as he passed, going up the three flights and bursting through the door.

"I didn't mean—" he started, his eleven-year-old face thin and pale like that of his father. Sofiya, wondering if someday her brother would be dry and wrinkled, shuddered and felt tenderness.

"Don't be afraid," she said, walking to Lev and guiding him to the kitchen and the sink. "Kostya was just frightened. He wasn't hurt so badly."

"I'm not scared," Lev protested, panting as he wet his face and drank warm tap water from his dirty cupped hands. "Did you hear what he called you?"

"He called me the name after you hit him. You didn't hit him because he called me a name," she said, helping Lev peel off his now-wet shirt to reveal a chest of bones.

"No, it was before," Lev insisted. "You think he'll get the police?"

"He won't get the police," Sofiya said, touching his head. Lev started to back away from her warm touch, then changed his mind and accepted it. She was much older than he, old enough to be his mother. His resentment, confusion, and love were as great as hers, and they brought brother and sister together.

"Kostya's uncle is in the KGB," Lev said, ferreting out a piece of bread from under the bread box. "Maybe he'll get mad and call his uncle on us."

"Kostya's uncle is not in the KGB." Sofiya sighed, scooping up crumbs from the table where he dropped them. "He's a stupid man who sells coffee in the Byelorussian Railway Station."

She poured him a glass of milk and told him to wash the sink.

"He in the tub again?" asked Lev, sitting at the small kitchen table. She nodded, affirming what he knew. Lev's breath was coming more slowly now.

"You have homework," Sofiya said.

Lev's dark face turned automatically sour, but the routine of homework was reassuring, so he went to the tiny bedroom he shared with his sister to fetch his books. Sofiya got her book and brought it to the table to sit with him.

The bathroom water pounded steadily behind them through the thin walls, washing concentration away, making the lines in the book become nonsense. Finally, the water stopped and she imagined Abraham turning the pages of *Izvestia* with displeasure. His presence was inescapable in the apartment, in her life.

The knock at the front door came firm and insistent, and Lev bolted upright in fear.

"It's the police," he said, knocking his milk over.

"It's probably Kostya and his mother," Sofiya said as calmly as she could, reaching over to clean up the milk with a rag. The prospect of Hania Shevchenko with her narrow eyes, sharp voice, and demands, made Sofiya bite her lip, but there was nothing to be done. Two boys had fought on a hot afternoon, and one had tasted his own blood and the hidden secret of his mortality. That taste had driven him to his mother, and her fear of mortality made her want to scream in anguish. It was a street ritual, and it required an audience, though no one expected any real action, for there was no real action to be taken. No one would call the Moscow police. Hania had the right, the obligation, to wail and be heard. Sofiya did not feel up to it, but she had no choice.

"Coming," she shouted as Lev scurried past her to their bedroom and closed the door.

Sofiya paused in the dark hall in front of the door to look at the two mounted photographs, one of her father and some friends in their youth, the other of her sad, smiling mother. Since her mother had died, Sofiya had never passed the photograph without looking at it. A few times she had gone to bed in the early weeks unsure of whether she had passed the photo without the required look, but on such nights Sofiya had gone quietly as she could to turn on the light and make her eyes meet those of her mother.

Now Sofiya sighed and opened the door, not to the wild figure of Hania Shevchenko but to two dark, heavy men, one as old as her father, the other young. They were shadow figures of a far country and dressed exactly alike, and they were, she was sure, neither the police nor the KGB. Sofiya had the strange impression that they were not two separate men but one man presented before her at two ages.

"Abraham Savitskaya," said the older man.

"He's taking a bath," Sofiya answered, her eyes moving from one man to the other.

The younger man said something to the older one in what Sofiya thought was English, and the old man, who had an ugly scar on his cheek, replied in the same tongue.

"Anyone here besides you and Savitskaya?" asked the old man.

"My little brother's in his room," she said, standing between the two men and the small apartment.

"If you want to wait for my father—" she began, but got no further. The younger man pushed her aside and drew from his pocket a huge gun that seemed to have a life of its own, pulling the young man behind it, searching corners. Sofiya staggered back a few steps with feelings she didn't understand. She was afraid but excited as the young man stepped toward her and aimed the gun over her shoulder at the bedroom door.

"No," she screamed. "That's my bedroom—my brother. He's just eleven."

The young man slapped her out of the way again and pushed open the bedroom door. She could see Lev sitting on the bed beyond, looking up in terror.

"Who're you talking to?" Abraham shouted down the hall from the bathroom.

"Pa," Sofiya screamed. She hobbled forward toward the bathroom, but the younger man grabbed her by the hair and punched her in the left breast, sending streaks of pain through her body as she fell. The bedroom door open, Lev ran out, fear in his eyes.

"Go back," Sofiya screamed, dragging herself toward her brother.

"What's going on?" shouted Abraham. Sofiya could hear the old man rising from his bath. She turned and pulled her useless leg to the hallway, a confused Lev clinging to her. Then the room and the world went into a series of still images she would never forget, snapshot images of the young dark man handing the gun to the old man. Then the image of the young man with his foot raised. Then the bathroom door kicked open. A blast of light and the memory of a terrible ringing echo. The blast repeated and repeated. She covered her ears and felt Lev's face buried against her sore breast, and then it was over. The two men came back to the small apartment, took something, gave Sofiya a warning glance, and left.

Sofiya and Lev sat huddled on the hall floor in shock forever. When forever passed, they stood hand in hand and moved into the hall toward the open door of the bathroom. They knew Abraham was dead before they saw his thin white arm sprawled awkwardly out of the tub and one gray foot twisted against the wall. His eyes were closed, but his mouth was angry, and *Izvestia* sank slowly in the red water. They stood looking down at the father they had never seen naked in life and were transported into a new world where time and life meant nothing.

"We'll have to clean the floor quickly," she said. "And then we'll have to call Comrade Tovyev and tell him about the broken door and then . . ." But her voice was no longer saying words; it had taken on a life of its own and was screaming louder than the echo of death.

"An old Jew's been shot in his bathtub on Balaklava Prospekt. Central desk has the house number."

The message had been given to Porfiry Petrovich Rostnikov over the phone. It was brief, informative, and carried far more than its message. Rostnikov had grunted and the new assistant procurator, Khabolov, hung up before Rostnikov could reply, "Yes, comrade."

The assistant procurator's words were a reminder that

Inspector Rostnikov was now reduced to handling insignificant Moscow murders and that one could mention "Jews" to him in a patronizing way. Rostnikov's wife, Sarah, was Jewish. The assistant procurator certainly knew this. If Sarah were not Jewish, Rostnikov himself would probably have been making the call to an inspector while he, Rostnikov, sat in the assistant procurator's chair in a small office with a cup of tea in his palms.

In Moscow, the investigation of a crime is a question of jurisdiction, and the investigation of important crimes is an important question of jurisdiction. Minor crimes, and no one is quite sure what a minor crime is, are handled at the inquiry stage by MVD, the national police with headquarters in Moscow. Moscow itself is divided into twenty police districts, each responsible for crime within its area. However, if a case is considered important enough, a police inspector from central headquarters will be assigned. The *doznaniye*, or inquiry, is based on the frequently stated assumption that "every person who commits a crime is punished justly, and not a single innocent person subjected to criminal proceedings is convicted." This is repeated so frequently by judges, procurators, and police that almost everyone in Moscow is sure it cannot be true. This assumption of justice is also made for military and state crimes handled by KGB investigators, who determine for themselves if the crime is indeed a state or military crime. Major nonmilitary crimes, however, are within the province of the procurator's investigator, who is responsible for a *predvaritel'noe sledstvie*, or preliminary police investigation.

All police officers in the system work for the procurator's office. The procurator general is appointed to his office for seven years, the longest term of any Soviet officer. Working under him or her are subordinate procurators, who are appointed for five years at a time. The job of the procurator's office is enormous: to sanction arrests, supervise investigations, oversee appeals at trials, handle execution of sentences, and supervise detention. The procurator general's office is police, district attorney, warden, and if necessary, executioner. The procurators of Moscow are very busy.

Rostnikov had stood behind his desk in a small cubbyhole office at the Central Petrovka station, straightened his left leg as best he could, and sighed deeply. The leg, partly crippled when he confronted a German tank in the battle of Rostov, had been giving him more trouble recently. Rostnikov catalogued the possible reasons for this increased aching. First, he was simply, at fifty-four, getting older, and with age came pain. Second, since the failure of his scheme to obtain exit visas for his wife and himself, he had spent more and more time working with his weights in their small apartment. The trophy he had won a month earlier gleamed bronze and small in front of him, and he found it easy to lose himself in the pain and the strain of the weights. One morning he had heard a uniformed duty officer say to another as he passed Rostnikov, "That washtub is looking a little washed out." Rostnikov did not object to being known as the Washtub. He rather liked it. What disturbed him was that he not only agreed with the assessment that he seemed washed out, but he took some comfort in it.

"Zelach," Rostnikov had called, throwing his jacket over his arm and going into the long, dark room outside his office. The room was modern, clean, filled with desks and men working behind them.

Zelach had looked up as if awakened from a mildly pleasant dream. He was reliable, slow of mind and foot, and the only help Rostnikov had been allowed since his informal demotion.

Zelach stood and followed. He had no curiosity and thus asked no questions as he followed Rostnikov down the aisle of desks past men at their solitary task of filling out reports. None of the actual interrogation was done out there. Interrogation, which could take hours or days if necessary, was normally carried on in small rooms down another corridor. The rooms could be made extremely warm or extremely cold, depending on the investigating officer's assessment of the subject or the witness.

Rostnikov did not try to divert his eyes from the third desk, the desk of Emil Karpo, who had nearly died a month earlier in an explosion in Red Square. Since his return to duty, his right arm lying limp in a black sling, Karpo had been even less communicative than before. Karpo, he thought, had a look of death in his eyes. It was, Rostnikov knew, an old man's thought, the thought that things were better in the past and would only get worse in the future.

"What?" said Zelach, now at his side as he passed the desk.

"I said nothing," said Rostnikov, though he was not at all sure that he had said nothing.

In front of Petrovka they hurried to the metro. Zelach had not, in the past month, appeared to notice that Rostnikov no longer had access to a car and driver or that the cases he was assigned were far below the level of social and political import of those in the past. In some ways, Rostnikov envied his lumbering assistant. *If you do not let the world in, if it seems unchanged, it can cause you no pain. Nichevo*, he thought, *nothing. Never let anything bother or surprise you. Be resolved to accept anything and nothing.*

As he dropped his five kopeks into the metro's turnstile slot, Rostnikov turned to Zelach. "What would you say if I were to tell you that you have been deemed a political liability and that I would have to shoot you in the next ten seconds?"

Zelach, instead of looking puzzled at the question, let a frightened-looking man in a workman's cap squeeze by them and then answered, "Good-bye, Comrade Rostnikov."

"As I thought," said Rostnikov, hearing a train rumble below them and rise to a roar that ended conversation.

On the escalator ride down, Rostnikov reflected for the thousandth time that he had been the victim of terrible timing and overconfidence.

The plan had been dangerous but simple, but chance, which should always be reckoned with, had laughed at him. Chance and accident had always played a part in the life of Steve Carella and the 87th Precinct, the American novels purchased on the black market that Rostnikov loved and kept hidden in his apartment behind the Russian classics and the collected speeches of Lenin.

Chance had failed to crown Rostnikov's plan. He had set up an elaborate blackmailing of a KGB senior officer named Drozhkin that involved Rostnikov's silence concerning the cover-up and the KGB assassination of a well-known dissident and Rostnikov's assurance that the official reports, which were with a friend in West Germany, would not be released if exit visas for Rostnikov and his wife were issued. It was to have been processed as a routine exit visa for a dissident Jew and her husband with special permission for a police officer to depart based on his years of loyal service in both the military and the government.

However, Brezhnev had died, and Andropov had taken over. Andropov had been a friend and admirer of Drozhkin's and when Andropov took over, Drozhkin had been promoted, which meant he spent more quiet days on his dacha in Lobnya. And then Andropov had died, followed quickly by Chernenko's death, which confused the situation even further. It had all gone wrong. Drozhkin had simply refused to deal with him. Rostnikov could have committed suicide by having the papers released in Germany to the Western press. As it was, there was still the threat of release, and at some level of the KGB apparently a decision had been informally or formally made. A stalemate existed. Rostnikov would not be allowed to leave the Soviet Union. However, he would not lose his job or be driven to complete despair, which might make him release the embarrassing report. It was a chess game in which the police officer had been outmaneuvered by the KGB. In this case, the stalemate had been a victory for the KGB.

In the rumbling metro Rostnikov looked over at a woman with an *avoska*, a string sack on her lap, and wondered briefly if his case had actually made it to the desk of Andropov. It was possible but not terribly likely. It would have made the situation more bearable for him to know that it had reached such a level.

More painful, however, was the knowledge that Rostnikov's son, Josef, who was serving his time in the army and stationed in Kiev, would certainly be part of the continuing stalemate. Were the papers to be released to *Stern* or the *New York* or *London Times*, Josef would be on the next plane to Afghanistan. That threat had been made explicit by Drozhkin.

"We're here," Zelach said, shouldering past a pair of young men with paper sacks under their arms. One of the younger men considered a look of anger, let his eyes take in the two disgruntled policemen, and changed his mind.

Rostnikov dragged his leg behind him and just managed to get through the door of the train and onto the platform of the Prospekt Vernadskogo station behind Zelach as the door closed. He glanced back into the passing train and caught a look of clear hatred from the now-safe young man within. Had the young man been within reach, Rostnikov probably would have lifted him off the ground and shaken him like a sack of grain.

"Zelach," he said as they rode up the escalator, "do you think of me as a violent man?"

"No, chief inspector," said Zelach indifferently. "There's a stand on the corner. I have not eaten. Would it be all right if I bought some blinchiki?"

"It would be all right, Comrade Zelach," Rostnikov said sarcastically, but the sarcasm was lost on Zelach. "Do you want to know where we are going?"

Zelach shrugged as they pressed through the morning crowd.

"In that case, we will let that be your surprise for the day."

In almost any country in the world, the knowledge that a murder had taken place would draw a crowd. In Naples, it would be almost impossible for the police to make their way through the crush of curious onlookers speculating on who had done what to whom and for what reasons. The situation would have been the same in Liverpool, Tokyo,

Cleveland, or Bern, but in Moscow the sidewalk in front of the tenement was clear. Curiosity was there, but it was overcome by the fear of becoming involved, questioned, asked to remember and comment, to be made part of an official report.

The building was one of the Stalin postwar blocks that looked like pale refrigerators. The apartments were usually dark, small, and far too hot in the summer. One could be easily disoriented by the sameness of such structures all over the city. Since Rostnikov's own apartment on Krasikov Street was from the same period and in the same style, although in a slightly better neighborhood, he was filled with a weary sadness as he followed Zelach through the door and into the small lobby.

There was no one there, no children, no old people. The building seemed deserted for a Wednesday evening, but both Rostnikov and Zelach were accustomed to this. Later, Zelach would wearily knock on doors and cajole, threaten, or force statements from people who insisted that they had seen and heard nothing.

"Floor?" Zelach asked.

"Three," said Rostnikov, moving to the stairwell. The trip up the concrete steps was slow due to Rostnikov's leg, and since their voices echoed unpleasantly, as in Lenin's tomb, they said nothing.

When Rostnikov opened the door on the third floor, a small girl, no more than four, stood staring at him. Her hair was braided behind her, and she sucked her thumb. Rostnikov smiled.

"*Oo menya temperatoora*," the little girl said, indicating that she had a temperature.

"I'm sorry to hear that," said Rostnikov.

"They killed the man with the beard," she said round her thumb.

"So I understand," said Rostnikov.

"Who are they?" the little girl asked, now taking her thumb from her mouth.

"We will see," said Rostnikov. Zelach stood, hands behind his back, patiently waiting for his superior to finish interrogating the child.

"Will they come back?" said the girl. Her eyes were so pale blue that they almost blended with the white and reminded Rostnikov of his own son as a child.

"They will not come back," Rostnikov assured her. "Did you see them?"

The girl shook her head no and glanced down the hall at a door that was now creaking open. An old woman dressed in black came out of the open door, looking quite frightened and stepping as if the floor were made of the shells of eggs.

"Elizaveta," the *babushka* whispered, not looking at the men. "Come now."

"No," the child said, looking coyly at Rostnikov.

"I think you should go, Elizaveta," Rostnikov said. "You have a temperature."

The girl giggled and ran to her grandmother, who snatched her in by the arm after giving an apologetic and very guilty look in the general direction of the two policemen. The door closed, and the men were alone again.

"You'll talk to the old woman later," Rostnikov said.

Zelach nodded, and they strode to the door of number 31. Rostnikov knocked and was answered almost immediately by a woman's voice.

"Yes," the voice said, strong, familiar, and in command.

Rostnikov knew who it was, and the knowledge drained him further.

"Inspector Rostnikov," he said, and the door opened to reveal the uniformed presence of Officer Drubkova, her face pink and eager, her zeal oppressive and tiring.

"Comrade inspector," she said, stepping back to let him in. "This is the victim's daughter and son, Sofiya and Lev Savitskaya. The victim is Abraham Savitskaya, eighty-three years. His body is still in the bath down the hall." She nodded with her head as Rostnikov and Zelach came in. Rostnikov caught the eyes of the no-longer young woman standing in the corner with one arm around a boy whose frightened eyes tried to take in everything at once, to keep everyone and all things in view so they could not get behind him. There was something about the woman that struck Rostnikov. It was like seeing for the first time a relative known only in childhood. If she were the victim's daughter, then she was at least half Jewish, and so, he thought, there may be some reminder of Sarah, but it went beyond that, and when she moved, he knew what it was.

The woman stepped forward as if to ask a question, and her limp was pronounced, quite similar to Rostnikov's own. Perhaps she had seen him move into the room and made the connection.

"Excuse me," she said.

Officer Drubkova, ever efficient, moved to the woman, probably to guide her back to the corner until the inspector was ready for her. Drubkova's firm hands took the woman's shoulders, but Sofiya Savitskaya did not turn away. The boy stayed back, eyes darting.

"It is all right, officer," Rostnikov said, shifting his coat to his other arm.

Zelach asked, indelicately, "You want me to go look at the corpse?"

Rostnikov nodded first at Zelach, who lumbered back into the hall, and then at the woman, who had limped forward.

"They killed my father," she said.

"We know," Rostnikov answered, and realized that he had one of the dazed ones, the ones for whom the trauma had been so great that they viewed violent events of the immediate past as if they were of no time, no place, just vague images they were trying to get to stop shimmering long enough to ask questions about their reality.

"The two men shot him," she said. The boy moved forward, frightened, to hold his sister's arm. If she were lost in madness, he would have no one.

"She will be all right," Rostnikov assured the boy. "This is one of the natural reactions. Why don't we all sit down. . . ."

"Lev," the boy said, holding his sister's arm firmly. "My name is Lev."

"Why don't we all sit down after you get me a drink of water," Rostnikov said, finding a kitchen chair and lowering himself into it. Lev considered whether there might be a trap in the request and then cautiously moved to the sink in the kitchen section of the room. Officer Drubkova watched the boy suspiciously, as if he might grab the glass of water and make a mad escape with it into the hall.

"Officer Drubkova," Rostnikov said, taking the glass of tepid water. "Find a phone and be sure the evidence truck is on the way. Comrade—"

"Her name is Sofiya," Lev said, leading his sister to a chair.

"Sofiya," Rostnikov said, sipping the water, "where is there a phone in this building?"

"There's one—" Lev began, but Rostnikov put a finger to his lips, and the boy stopped.

"Comrade Sofiya?" Rostnikov repeated to the staring woman. "A phone. I need help here."

Sofyka made an effort to refocus, came back into the world temporarily, and said, "Thirty-three, Vosteksky has a phone."

Officer Drubkova nodded and went in search of the phone, closing the door behind her.

"Your father is dead," Rostnikov said to the two in front of him. The boy was now standing, holding his sister, his hands on her shoulders. "And we should like to find out who killed him and why. Do you have an answer to either question?"

"Two men," said Lev. "A young one and a very old one like—"

"Like me," finished Rostnikov.

"No, older, like my, my—"

"And you have never seen them before?" Rostnikov said, finishing the water and putting the glass on the table, which was covered with a slightly worn flower-patterned tablecloth made from some oilclothlike material.

"Never," said Lev.

"And you, Sofiya? You have never seen them before?" Rostnikov said gently.

"I've seen the old one," she said, looking through Rostnikov into eternity.

"Good." Rostnikov sighed with a gentle smile, thinking that perhaps he could wrap all this up and get home before ten for a decent dinner. "He is a neighbor, a friend, an old enemy?"

Sofiya glanced around the room as if looking for someone or something and then brought her puzzled glance back to Rostnikov. Her answer made him revise his plans for a reasonable dinnertime and the possibility of an hour of weightlifting before the hockey match on his little television.

"I don't know where, but I've seen him, but it wasn't quite him. Do you know what I mean?"

"Exactly," Rostnikov said reassuringly, though he had no idea of what she meant. "Try to remember where you have seen him. Now, your father, what was his business, his work?"

"He didn't work," Lev said, and Rostnikov thought there was a touch of something, perhaps resentment, in the words.

"He was ill," Sofiya jumped in. "He used to be in the Party, but when my mother died, I don't know how long ago, he became ill and didn't work. I work. I teach children at the Kalinina School. I teach reading, shorthand, and—"

"Did your father talk about enemies?" Rostnikov put in before she could launch into an irrelevant discussion of the Soviet educational system.

"He imagined many enemies," Lev said. "Mostly the police, the KGB, others."

"Imagined?"

"He claimed he had an old friend in the government," Sofiya said. "Someone who was having him watched."

"And you think that might have been true?" Rostnikov asked.

"No," Sofiya said. "He lied a lot."

She seemed on the verge of crying, which was all right with Rostnikov, but he had information to get, and he would prefer to get it before she began. Then he would even help her to cry, throw her some cue that would set her free to moan and rejoin the world, but he wanted to do that as he left, after he had drained her of information. Anything else was wasteful.

"Did these men take anything?" Rostnikov asked, turning his attention to Lev, whose hand had come to his mouth as if to hold back a cry. The eyes continued to scan, but more slowly now. He was becoming a bit more calm.

"I don't know," the boy said, looking around the not very spacious and not overly filled room. "Sofie?"

The woman shook her head to indicate that she did not know.

Rostnikov stood up with some difficulty. "Why don't you look around and let me know. I'll go down the hall and come back."

"How did you injure your leg?" the woman asked.

"War," answered Rostnikov, draping his jacket over the chair he had vacated to make it clear to them that he was coming right back. "When I was a boy not much older than your brother. And you?"

"I was born with it," she said, shuddering. "My father and mother gave it to me as a birthday present. You know I loved my father?"

"I can see that," Rostnikov said, moving as quickly as he could to the door.

"I did, too," said Lev, a bit defiantly.

"Did you?" asked Rostnikov, opening the door. He suddenly felt hungry and cursed the fact that he had not joined Zelach in a quick blinchik or two.

"No," said Sofiya, her eyes challenging. "I did not love him. I hated him."

"I understand," said Rostnikov.

"And I loved him."

"I understand that, too," he said to her gently, going out into the hall.

The wood of the door was thin. He expected a loud wail

when he closed it, but instead he heard gentle sobbing. He had to strain to determine which of the two was crying and knew with certainty only when he heard the woman's voice. "Shh, Lev. Shh. We will be fine."

The door to the communal bathroom was open, and Officer Drubkova was now guarding it.

"I called in," she greeted him. "They will be here in minutes."

Rostnikov grunted and stepped past her, resisting the urge to compliment her or say something pleasant. The Officer Drubkovas of the MVD were sustained by efficiency and self-satisfaction, a belief that those above them were above human feeling, images of an idealized Lenin. To compliment Drubkova would have been to diminish himself in her eyes.

Zelach was on his knees in front of the old tub, which looked as if it had belonged to a relative of the czar's. It stood on clawed legs that gripped metal balls pitted with age and wear. Zelach had found a towel and placed it on the floor for his knee. He was methodically examining the grotesque body in the tub without emotion, concentrating on his task.

For a moment Rostnikov took in the scene. The water was almost orange with blood, and the sticky remnant of *Izvestia* quivered just below the surface. Rostnikov could see a photograph on the front page, though he could not, through the orange film, make out who it was. The dead old man was very thin and very white. One arm hung out of the tub, pointing down at the tile floor. The other was under the water, hidden, touching a secret place or thing. The old man's chest was thin and covered with wisps of gray hair. Two black holes in his chest peeked through, caked with blood. The old man's face was gray bearded and, like that of the boy, thin. The features were regular, and even in death there was something about him that said, "I've been cheated. You, anyone who comes near me, are out only for one thing, to cheat me out of something that is my own."

"And?" said Rostnikov.

"Shot," said Zelach.

"I am surprised." Rostnikov, sitting on the closed toilet seat, sighed.

"No, look, the bullet holes are quite evident—" Zelach began. Rostnikov put his head down and almost whispered, "I see, Zelach. I see. I was attempting to engage in a bit of humor. Levity."

"Ah, yes," said Zelach, anxious to please but not understanding. "Yes, it was amusing." He either chuckled or began to choke. Rostnikov, taking no chances, leaned over to pat the man's back, which resulted in Zelach's bumping into the dangling arm of the corpse, which set off a small chain reaction. The balance of the corpse changed, and Abraham Savitskaya's body began to sink below the surface of the reddish water.

"What should I—?" Zelach said hopelessly.

Rostnikov didn't care. He shrugged, and Zelach reached over to grab the corpse's sparse gray hair. He was pulling the body out by the hair as Officer Drubkova stuck her head in to announce that the evidence truck had arrived. If the sight of the kneeling officer pulling a corpse's hair revolted, surprised, or shocked her, she gave no indication. She simply made her announcement and backed away to let in a man and a woman, both wearing suits, both carrying small suitcases, both serious. Rostnikov recognized the two of them, Comrades Spinsa and Boritchky, a team who spoke little, worked efficiently, and reminded him of safecrackers in a French movie.

"He is already dead," said Boritchky, a small man of about sixty. "You need not redrown him, Zelach."

Zelach let go of the corpse's hair and stood up. The body did, this time, sink under.

"Thank you," said Comrade Spinsa, herself about fifty, very thin with prominent, pouting underlip. "Now we shall have to drain the tub for even the beginning of an examination."

"I didn't—" Zelach began, looking over to Rostnikov on the toilet seat for support.

Rostnikov's mind was elsewhere. Zelach was not worth

saving from embarrassment. Rostnikov had better uses for his energy.

"We'll leave you alone," Rostnikov said, getting up. "Zelach will check with you when you're done. How long?"

Boritchky moved to the tub, considered how to let the water out without getting his sleeve bloody red, and announced over his shoulder that they would be done in about twenty minutes.

Officer Drubkova took a step down the hall with Rostnikov and Zelach, but Rostnikov held up a hand to stop her.

"Under no circumstances," Rostnikov said, "is anyone not associated with police business to enter that bathroom. You are to remain and see to this."

"Yes, comrade," she said firmly.

Having gotten rid of her, Rostnikov limped back to the Savitskaya apartment with Zelach behind, mumbling an apology.

"Quiet," said Rostnikov as he opened the apartment door.

"Otets?" said Sofiya Savitskaya expectantly.

"Your father is indeed dead," Rostnikov said.

Brother and sister were in the same position he had left them. Rostnikov considered bringing them down to Petrovka, but the case really didn't warrant that attention.

"Did you remember where you have seen the older man who killed your father, and is anything missing?"

"The candlestick," said Lev. "They took my grandmother's brass candlestick."

"A brass candlestick." Rostnikov sighed, picking up his coat. "Zelach will get a description. Why would someone want your grandmother's brass candlestick?"

"And the old man?"

"In the hall," Sofiya said, looking up. "I've seen him in the hall. Every day for years, in the hall."

She was looking up at Rostnikov, still dazed.

"He lives in this building, works in this building?"

She shook her head no.

"Then . . . ?"

"The photograph," she said, pointing to the little alcove off of the door. Rostnikov turned around and found himself facing two photographs. One was of a woman. Rostnikov concluded that she must, this kerchief-headed, sad-looking woman, be the dead wife of the recently dead man in the tub. Next to this photograph was another, of five men in peasant dress. Four of the men were very serious. All were young, and the picture was clearly old. Rostnikov moved to it and looked at the quartet with arms around each other's shoulders. Rostnikov thought that one looked vaguely like a young version of the dead man. The look of suspicion was there, coming through a weak, pale half smile. Only one of the five in the photo, a man younger than the rest, was truly grinning.

"Which one?" Rostnikov said. Zelach was right behind him, peering at the picture.

"The man who smiles," Sofiya said. "It was him."

"You are sure?"

"I'm sure," she said.

"And who is he?"

"I don't know. I don't know who any of them are. He never told us."

Without asking, Rostnikov took the picture from the wall and handed it to Zelach. He wasn't at all sure that the woman wasn't having a delusion or creating a tale, connecting a man in the hall who had helped kill her father with a photograph in the hall from her dead father's past.

"Lev," Rostnikov said, turning into the room. "Do you agree? Was the man in the picture the one who came here this afternoon?"

The boy looked at his sister, whose head was down and whose hands were in her lap and said, "Yes, it is him."

The boy's face turned to Rostnikov and belied his words. His face said he wasn't at all sure.

"Comrade Zelach will remain here and take more complete statements from you," Rostnikov said, improvising this way to avoid Zelach's company back to his office.

"Comrade Zelach will be most patient with you. Remember that, Zelach."

Zelach nodded glumly, but Rostnikov was sure that he would obey.

Rostnikov retrieved his jacket and took one final look at the brother and sister, wondering if he could say something, do something, to help them get through the night, but there was nothing. He could say that he would find the killer, but he doubted if they really cared. He was sure that the assistant procurator and the procurator did not care. It was doubtful, in fact, if anyone with the exception of Chief Inspector Porfiry Petrovich Rostnikov really cared, and, in truth, he didn't care very much, either.

Still, the nibble of a question began to get at him. Why would anyone murder for a brass candlestick? Was the man in the photograph from Savitskaya's past really the one who had come to shoot him? Why?

He was thinking about such things, finding himself beginning to get lost in a possible puzzle, when a fat woman, hands on her hips, appeared before him on the narrow steps.

"Did you arrest him?"

"Arrest who?"

"The Jewish boy," she said. "He threw my son down the steps this afternoon. He is a wild one. He deserves to be arrested, punished."

Rostnikov managed to ease past her and looked back over his shoulder at the woman on the steps.

"Don't worry, comrade. He is being punished."

TWO

EMIL KARPO STOOD IN FRONT OF THE STATUE OF FIELD Marshal Kutuzov, commander of the Russian army in the War of 1812, but he did not look at the statue or at the Triumphal Arch at the end of Kutuzovsky Prospekt that commemorated the heroes of that same war with the French. As far as Karpo was concerned, it was a decadent war fought by two imperialist forces. It was far better that the Russian imperialists won. It was not, however, something to build monuments to, though he understood the sense of history necessary to unite the Russian people.

Emil Karpo was only slightly aware that more people were looking at him as he stood almost motionless than at the portly stone general seated on his horse twenty feet above him. Few looked directly at Karpo as they headed for the Panorama Museum of the Battle of Borodino, but few failed to notice the tall, lean, and pale figure dressed in black with his right hand tucked under his jacket as if he were reaching for a hidden gun or mocking that Napoleon whom the Great Mikhail Kutuzov had thwarted more than 170 years earlier. Some thought the tall, pale man looked like a vampire whose dark wing had been broken. One couple considered his resemblance to the painting of a Tatar that stood inside the Pushkin Museum of Fine Arts. A tourist named Marc Lablancet from Lyon considered taking a photograph of Karpo in front of the statue, but his wife tugged at him and hurried him away.

The cars and buses beeped, braked, and chugged noisily

around the Triumphal Arch, but Karpo paid no attention. A passing group of Japanese tourists simply assumed the pale man was mad or meditating; in fact, they were quite close to the truth. Karpo never gave a label to his moments and even hours of concentration. He simply lost himself in the problem to which he had been assigned. His logic was unquestionable. He was a policeman. His job was to prevent crime or bring to justice those who committed a crime. Any crime was a threat to the state, an indication that the criminal did not respect the Party, the Revolution, and the need for total dedication. If there was any meaning to existence for Karpo, it was that the commonweal must be respected, sustained. His dedication to Leninist communism was complete, though he did not see Lenin as a god. Lenin had been a man, a man dedicated to the eventual establishment of a world as close to perfection for all as would be possible, given the weaknesses of the animal that was man.

Little more than a month earlier, Emil Karpo had stopped a terrorist from damaging and possibly destroying Lenin's tomb. Karpo expected no reward for his action. Indeed, the government had even covered up the incident and labeled the bomb damage in Red Square "a gas-line explosion." Karpo had awakened days after the incident to face an incompetent doctor who told him he would soon have the use of his right hand again if he engaged in the proper therapy. The woman had spoken with confident calm as she stood over his bed, but one of the several weaknesses of the system that Karpo recognized and expected to see changed was the low level of competence of physicians.

Karpo had not even bothered to nod his acknowledgment at the porcine woman. She had made the mistake of trying to wait him out, but he simply stared at her for five minutes, and she left in angry defeat. Two weeks later he left the hospital and ignored Rostnikov's suggestion that he see a doctor who might know what he was talking about.

"My wife's cousin," Rostnikov had said, looking at Karpo's arm. "He'll look at you. He's good, Jewish."

Karpo had declined, abruptly indicating his confidence in the system. In his small monastic room each night Karpo had attempted the exercises suggested by the hospital therapist, but they did no good. There was no doubt in Karpo's mind that he would never regain the use of his right arm, and so instead of continuing the useless therapy, he had spent silent hours teaching himself to be left-handed. Left-handedness was discouraged in Russia. Russian children caught using their left hand to throw, write, or eat were sternly stopped. Karpo had never thought much about this, assuming the idea of conformity was simply part of one's education in an overpopulated society. But now Karpo had to become left-handed. He wrote slowly, carefully, in his notebooks, his private volumes of detailed reports on every case to which he was assigned. He wrote about the new case to which he had been assigned and wondered why it had been given to him and not to his superior, Porfiry Petrovich Rostnikov. He wondered but did not speak of his wonder as he learned to write with his left hand and constructed the details about the sniper who was shooting at people from the rooftops in Central Moscow.

There had been five shootings, three resulting in death. There had been no real clues besides the bullets, with the possible exception of the report by the drunken night porter of the Ukraine Hotel who swore that he heard someone weeping loudly on the roof of the hotel on the night of the third shooting. Since the bullets had certainly come from the hotel roof, the sniper had been given the nickname the Weeper, but it was a nickname only a few in Petrovka shared. No word of the snipings had been heard on the radio or television, and no reports had appeared in the press.

The Weeper would go on killing without the people of Moscow knowing of it until he or she was caught or the shootings became pandemic. It was, Karpo was sure, better this way. There was nothing to be gained from alerting the public to this crime. There were no safeguards to be taken. There was nothing to do except catch the sniper and turn him over for a quiet trial, or perhaps no trial at all.

So Karpo had learned to drink his black tea with his left hand, to dress himself with his left hand, and to write his clear, precise notes with his left hand. Deep within him, as he adjusted to the change, he considered what might happen if the procurator learned that his disability was permanent. It was inevitable, but until that inevitable moment came, he would continue to work as he had for twenty-two of his forty-three years.

And so it was that on a hot August morning Emil Karpo stood in front of the statue below the general and in front of the pedestal on which were carved life-sized images of the commanders, soldiers, and partisans who had long ago risen to the defense of their country.

Twenty minutes after he had taken up his vigil in the square, Karpo saw the man he had been waiting for. The man was about sixty, wearing a dark and slightly shabby hotel uniform. In his right hand was a small cloth sack. Instead of joining the flow of tourists, the man sought out a bench, found an empty seat, and looked around, squinting against the sun. Not finding what or who he was looking for, he opened his sack lovingly and removed a sandwich wrapped in newspaper and a small box from which he began to remove dominoes. An overweight woman on the far end of the bench who had stopped to catch her breath, a task she might never accomplish, glanced at the old man, who appeared to be offering her a game. Karpo could see the man's mouth moving and the woman nodding her head no as he left the statue and moved forward.

Karpo brushed by a couple trying to figure out a visitor's map and approached the bench, standing between the old man and the sun, throwing his shadow over the black dominoes the man was placing on the bench. The fat woman looked at Karpo and forced herself up, pretending to see someone she knew. Karpo ignored the open space on the bench and stood over the man, who looked up at the dark outline before him.

"A game?" the man said. His teeth were in bad condition, but he was clean-shaven and, in spite of the hot weather, not nearly as rancid as many who worked in heavy uniforms were in the summer.

"Pavel Mikiyovich?" Karpo asked, though he knew this was the man.

Mikiyovich squinted up curiously, then with fear, and then with Moscow indifference, feigned and protective.

"I know you?" he asked.

"Inspector Karpo. Police."

Two little girls, about ten or eleven, in matching school dresses strolled by arm in arm and giggled at the two men, whispering.

"It's just dominoes," Mikiyovich said, holding up a double two to prove his point. "I'm not gambling."

"The man who wept," Karpo said. "The sniper."

Mikiyovich let out a small sigh of relief and gummed a bite of sandwich.

"I told the other man from the police everything," Mikiyovich said, looking at his sandwich, the tiles, anything to avoid the tall man who blocked the sun. "I'm on my lunch break. I've only got—"

"I was told I could find you here," Karpo interrupted. Karpo had read the report of the interview. It had been brief, and had he any other reasonable leads, he would not have bothered with this requestioning, at least not yet, but the chance existed that a new lead might arise.

Mikiyovich shrugged, resigned. He wondered if the man above him had only one arm or was scratching his stomach.

"He wept," Mikiyovich said, raising his arms, the remnant of sandwich in one hand, a domino in the other. "I was getting some air on the roof at nine."

"You went to the roof to drink," Karpo corrected.

"Never," Mikiyovich said indignantly.

"You had been warned about getting drunk on duty, so you went up to the roof," Karpo went on. "If you lie to me again, we go to Petrovka for a talk."

"I went to the roof to drink," the man said, shifting himself inside of his slightly oversized uniform.

"And," Karpo prompted.

Behind them on the Prospekt a Zaporozhets-968 automobile tried to pass a bus and caught a piece of the bus's rear fender. Bus driver and car driver raised their fists at each other, and the car sped on.

"There's nothing to tell," Mikiyovich said, sighing. "In the dark I heard something, a snap, something, maybe a gunshot, maybe not. It came from the far end of the roof overlooking the front of the hotel."

"You saw nothing?" Karpo said.

"Nothing," Mikiyovich said, shaking his head firmly to emphasize his lack of information. "Too dark and I was not curious. I am not a coward. I was in the army. I have a medal for the Battle of Leningrad."

"And you knew Lenin," Karpo said without a trace of sarcasm.

"I saw him once when I was a boy," the man said proudly.

"I do not doubt that you are a hero," Karpo said. "What did you hear?"

"Crying, just crying."

"Man or woman?"

"Who knows?"

"Guess," Karpo prodded, moving slightly so the sun would fall directly on the man as he tried to look up at the policeman.

"A man," Mikiyovich said.

"Old, young?"

"More young than old," the man said. "I'm guessing."

"Big or small man?" Karpo went on.

"Big or small—how should I know? Can I see in the darkness?"

"Did it sound like a big or small man? The weeping, any movement."

"A regular man," the old man said. "He wept. He coughed. A regular man."

"He coughed?" Karpo asked.

"He coughed," Mikiyovich agreed, coughing to demonstrate how insignificant the sound was.

"What kind of cough?"

"What kind of cough?" the old man repeated as if he were talking to a madman but remembering that this was a police madman. "I don't—"

"Deep, the cough of a smoker, a sick cough?"

"The first time a little cough, more like clearing the throat, and the second time a cough like when you have the grippe. Who can remember such things?"

"You remembered," Karpo said, turning his back and walking away.

Mikiyovich shrugged his shoulders and watched the policeman move down the walk with the crowd. A shudder ran down the old man's back, and he prayed to the unknown god that one was no longer supposed to believe in that the wounded bat of a policeman never returned to blot out the sun again. He started to take a bit of his sandwich, changed his mind, threw the remains in his bag, packed up his dominoes, and hurried to a state store where he still might be able to buy a bottle of kvass before his lunch break was over.

While Porfiry Petrovich Rostnikov was beginning to consider the facts in the case of the murder of the old Jew in the bathtub and Emil Karpo was questioning the hotel porter, Sasha Tkach was engaged in the investigation of a crime of far less moment than murder. Sasha had been selected for this investigation by the new assistant procurator because Sasha did not look like a policeman. At twenty-eight, he looked like a tall, young student. With the new clothes that had been provided for him, he looked like a prosperous young university student. His looks belied his feelings.

Sasha's wife, Maya, was about to have a baby, and they feared the consequences of living in those two rooms with a child and Sasha's mother, Lydia, who was becoming more and more difficult with each day. He could not afford to pay enough *nalevo*, money on the side, to get a new apartment. Now he stood in front of an old building that looked as if it had once been a barn, on a small street just off of Volgograd Prospekt. He had taken the Zhadanovsko-

Krasnopresnenskaya line of the metro to the Tekstilshchiki station and walked the five blocks, pausing to check off the name of the shop in his notebook even before he arrived.

His task was simple and boring, to visit every known automobile repair shop in the Moscow area, both the officially listed ones and those operated unofficially. For a city the size of Moscow, the list was quite small. For an individual taking the metro in the August heat, the list was monumental.

For almost four months, a well-organized team of automobile thieves had been focusing on the cars of the very rich, the very powerful. Normally, car theft in Moscow was routine; no part of a car was even safe overnight. Drivers routinely unscrewed outside mirrors and lamps and removed windshield wipers. Complaints were frequent, but the police had more important things to do, at least until this new gang had boldly gone into operation. They had begun by stealing two black Volgas belonging to politicians of more than moderate influence. A few months later, a black Chaika had been stolen from in front of the dacha of a member of the KGB not far from the Outer Ring Road. The Chaika had belonged to an admiral. So rare are these cars that the center VIP lane of major thoroughfares, reserved for government use, are known as "Chaika Lanes." The final blow, however, came when a black Zil limousine, the hand-tooled car that no more than two dozen members of the Politburo and a few national secretaries of the Communist Party owned, disappeared from in front of the apartment building where the then-acting head of the KGB resided. It was forcefully and officially denied to an English journalist who heard about the theft that the auto belonged to the distinguished old gentleman, but whoever it belonged to, the Zil, complete with armchair seats, air conditioning, telephones, and a bar, was gone.

The question of who might be buying these automobiles—the Zil alone would bring about $125,000 if someone dared purchase it—remained unanswered. The procurator general, however, had moved the investigation to high priority, higher than at least forty outstanding murders and a major drug ring. The highest priority, however, was given to keeping anyone from finding out about these bold and embarrassing thefts. So, boring though it might be, Tkach's task was deemed an important one. His charge had been simple and probably impossible.

"Find these enemies of the state before they steal one more vehicle essential for the security of our government," Assistant Procurator Khabolov had told him. And now Tkach stood in front of a building that had once been a barn.

Sasha Tkach, who had never owned a car and had seldom driven one, stepped through the side door next to the large corrugated and firmly closed steel sliding door and entered the shop.

He found himself standing in front of a wooden counter in a small customer area. The counter was covered with small pieces of metal, some of it oily but much of it rusting into the wooden counter like ancient fossils. Beyond the counter was a small open space with a concrete floor. On the floor were various unidentifiable pieces of machinery of sizes ranging from that of a coffee cup to what looked like a truck engine. A metallic buzzing filled the ill-lighted space, vibrating up Sasha's back and down his arms.

"Hello," he shouted.

The figure in a gray bulky one-piece work suit huddled over the piece of machinery on the floor paid no attention and continued to attack the mass of metal with a whirring tool that sent up sparks.

Remember who you are supposed to be, Sasha told himself, and he shouted again, louder, pounding a fist on the counter. Small pieces of unembedded metal jiggled and danced around his fist, and the figure with the whirring machine turned to face him, eyes hidden behind goggles. The figure turned off the machine.

"What?" said the man in a surly voice to the perspiring policeman.

"I want to talk," Sasha said.

"Talk," said the man without removing his goggles.

"It is confidential," Sasha went on. "Your name was

given to me by a friend who did not wish his name to be used."

The man stood up now and removed his goggles, letting them dangle around his neck. His face was grimy and his body huge and hulking.

"A man?" he said, slowly getting to his feet. He walked to the counter to look at Sasha and placed the heavy electric tool on the counter with a thud.

"A man you would know," Sasha said, lowering his voice confidentially.

"My name is Nikolai Penushkin," Sasha said, emphasizing the surname, which was that of a reasonably well-known member of the Politburo. "My father is . . . someone whose name I am sure you know."

The man's face was dark, covered with grime. "Your father sent you to me?" the man said.

"No," Sasha corrected slowly. "A friend sent me. A friend who thought you might be able to help me locate a car."

"A car?"

"To buy," Sasha said.

"You want to buy a car?"

"Yes," Sasha said, happy that some progress was being made. "A very good car. I can pay in rubles or even American dollars if necessary."

"I don't sell cars," the man said.

"My friend said that you might know someone who sold cars, very good cars," Sasha pushed. The man was not gifted with great intelligence.

"I know someone who sells cars," the grimy giant agreed.

"I would like a very fine car," Sasha said slowly, as if talking to a child. "A Zil, a black Zil."

"I—I've never been close to a Zil," he said. "Why are you coming to me? I have a little shop. I couldn't even touch a Zil. You have important friends—"

"Ah," said Sasha, now whispering. "But there are no Zils available. I heard that one was . . . missing and that you might know the person who found it and that the person who found it might be willing to part with it for the right price."

The big man studied Sasha's face for a few seconds, and the policeman tried to look like a spoiled son of an influential father. He grinned into the huge dark face and was about to speak again when a massive paw shot out and grabbed his tie. Sasha felt himself being strangled as the big man lifted him over the wooden counter. Sasha's feet clanked against the electric tool and over bits of metal.

"Idle parasites of the rich," the man whispered. "The state is being strangled by *nakhlebniki* like you. Your fathers struggle to make a world built on the bodies of those who died in the Revolution, and you drag us down."

The man had pushed Tkach against the corrugated steel door, which rattled behind him.

"No," Tkach managed to croak when the man put him down but didn't release his grip on the policeman's tie.

"I'll give you a lesson your father should have given you when you were a child," the giant said.

Tkach managed to reach under his jacket with his left hand and fumbled his pistol out with an awkward twist. The giant paid no attention. His eyes, brown and deep, were fixed on Tkach's. He was about to push his open palm against the policeman's nose when Tkach stuck the pistol in his face, aimed at the man's right eye.

Instead of dropping him, the huge man smiled. "I'll eat that gun," he said.

"I'm a policeman," Tkach said, gasping. In another second, he would either have to shoot this innocent lout or take a beating.

The man clearly didn't believe Tkach would shoot. He had heard too much of the cleverness of the idle rich. The man, whose name was Vadim, thought Sasha Tkach would never learn it, knew he was not himself clever, but he had faith in his instincts.

"I'll show you my identification card," Tkach said, still holding the pistol in front of the brown eye.

Vadim hesitated, and Tkach, still holding the gun, reached in with his free hand to pull out his identification card. He held it in front of Vadim's face and prayed that the man could read.

"So," said Vadim, not letting go, "you are a corrupt policeman trying—"

"To catch automobile thieves," Tkach finished. "I'm going to every repair shop, every dealer, every—"

The man hesitated, shook his head, and put Tkach down.

Sasha, his eyes still on the mechanic, slowly put his identification card and his gun away.

"If you have any idea of who might . . ." Sasha began talking through a rasping throat and adjusting his tie, but Vadim had already put his goggles on and had stepped away to reach for his tool. Sasha stopped talking and edged toward the counter as the man picked up the tool and turned it on. The whirring was deafening. It struck Sasha that the giant might decide to turn the swirling blade on his visitor. Before that could happen, Sasha took four steps across the floor, scrambled over the counter, and went through the door into the street where he took in three deep drafts of hot summer air and cursed the day he had ever decided to be a policeman.

When the waiter in restaurant number four of the massive Hotel Rossiya reached for the odd package on the table, a hand clamped his wrist, squeezing feeling from his fingers.

The waiter's name was Vladimir Kuznetsov, and until this moment he had been having a good day. He had a pocketful of change in tips from the French, Canadian, Italian, and American businessmen and tourists he had served, and in a few hours he would be off for a one-week vacation. There was not much to Vladimir Kuznetsov. He was a thin sparrow of a creature whose needs were small and ambitions even smaller. At present, his sole goal in life was to free himself from the viselike fingers around his wrist.

Kuznetsov had just deposited two plates of pickled fish in front of the two sullen foreigners who had been drinking for an hour like native Muscovites, but they were not Muscovites; Vladimir was sure of that.

The younger of the two men, who had grabbed his now-senseless wrist, said some nonsense in English that sounded like "Kipyur hans hoff."

The very old man looked at Vladimir but showed no emotion. He took a drink of vodka, pulled the long, wrapped package out of the waiter's reach, and said something in English to the younger man, who finally let Vladimir go.

"Forgive us," said the old man in Russian, but a Russian that sounded old, unused, and tinged with another accent that sounded American. The old man displayed no look of regret on his face. His eyes, instead, were far away or long ago.

"I understand," Vladimir said, resisting the urge to massage his feeling-deprived hand and wrist. He would not give the Americans the satisfaction. On the other hand, he decided not to insult them. Everyone knew Americans were mad, violent, but having behaved with violence, they often responded with guilty generosity. These were well-dressed men with money. A sizable tip might be in order.

Vladimir walked off slowly, with, he felt, dignity. He weaved his way around the tables, filled with people, most of whom were in military uniforms. He paused inside the door to the kitchen and looked back across the dining room at the two men at the table. Only at that point did Vladimir rub his wrist and look at it, pulling back the cuff of his frayed white shirt. Through the small window in the door, Vladimir could see that the old man had forgotten his fish and had laid his hand on the package Vladimir had been punished for almost touching. The younger man ate, but he kept his eyes respectfully on the old man, who was saying something.

Misha Kvorin was smoking as he leaned against the wall behind Vladimir. The two were not exactly friends, though they had known each other for more than ten years. Misha had the sour, sagging face of a pike.

Misha, looking, as always, bored, pushed himself from

the wall, pulled down his black jacket, and slouched toward the door to look over Vladimir's shoulder across the room.

"The two at eighteen," Vladimir said. "The old one and the mean-looking one. You see—you see that thing wrapped on the table?"

"I see," Misha said with a little cough.

"What do you think it is?"

"A package," Misha said, turning away.

"I tried to move it out of the way, and the younger one grabbed my wrist. I had to almost twist his arm off to make him let go."

"So?" said Misha, stepping aside so another waiter, almost as old as the old man at the table, could get past and out the door with a tray of zakuski.

"So," Vladimir said, "we should tell the police when they leave."

Misha gave a small and not amused laugh. "You want to go to the police? Who goes to the police, about anything? What do the police do? And this, over this? A package a foreigner won't let you touch? A package he puts right out on the table in plain sight?"

"But—"

"What do you think is in it? A shotgun?" Misha laughed, searching for his cigarettes. "Drugs? The severed limb of a Politburo member?"

"At least we should tell Comrade Tukanin," Vladimir tried again. Comrade Tukanin was the party organizer for the kitchen workers. He had the reputation of being more eager than any other group leader in the massive hotel. That's what he would do after the Americans were gone. He would make out a report to Tukanin. Maybe it would lead to the Americans being questioned by the police, made to feel uncomfortable or frightened. And who knows, maybe the two Americans did have something in that package they shouldn't have had.

Vladimir brushed past Misha, who gave him a look that made it clear Misha thought Vladimir was a pain in the face.

As it turned out, Vladimir got a ruble from the Americans and decided that filling out a report might delay his vacation or result in his being called back early to discuss his suspicions. Deep down he knew he had never really intended to file a complaint. Grumbling was one thing, action quite another.

And so Vladimir Kuznetsov never did find out that wrapped inside the paper between his two Americans was a cheap, heavy brass candlestick.

THREE

ROSTNIKOV DIDN'T GET HOME TO HIS APARTMENT ON Krasikov Street till almost eight. He had spent the day on the case of the old Jew who had been murdered. Normally, other cases, problems, requests, needs, public testimony, would take up his time, intrude so that a murder like this would drag on and probably be forgotten. But Rostnikov had plenty of time and no distractions, since the assistant procurator was keeping him isolated from the mainstream of activity at Petrovka.

From the records he could check and a few phone calls, Rostnikov had discovered that Abraham Savitskaya had been born in the village of Yekteraslav in 1902. Savitskaya had immigrated to the United States in 1917, just as the Revolution had begun. He had returned to Russia in 1924. Somehow Savitskaya had been given a series of minor but secure positions on the fringe of the Party. For six years he had been a clerk with the Soviet War Veterans Committee. After that he had been listed for almost a dozen years as a caretaker for the Committee for Physical Culture and Sport of the USSR Council of Ministers. In 1935, at the age of thirty-three, Abraham had been retired with a pension as the result of disability. Rostnikov had not been able to discover the nature of the disability. It was a slightly peculiar background, but Rostnikov had encountered life stories far more peculiar.

At the scarred desk in his small office, Rostnikov had stared at the photograph of the four men in a small village taken sixty-five years ago. There was so little of the dead old man in the photograph that he wondered how anyone could possibly identify one of the other men all these years later as Sofiya Savitskaya had done. They were probably all dead. The life expectancy of Russians was not officially published, but it was surely less than seventy-five years. Only the best-fed men in the government and the primitives in the Caucasus who stuffed themselves with goat milk and runny yogurt lived that long.

After a few minutes, the four young men in the picture began to look familiar to Rostnikov. First, the one on the left, the thinnest, with the cap, reminded Rostnikov of one of the men who swept the halls in Petrovka on alternate nights. The man next to him looked suspiciously like the famous clown Popoff, though Popoff was now almost two decades younger than the man in the photograph. Rostnikov had taken the photograph and left it for Zelach to have copies made. It was possible Rostnikov would never get the photograph back, let alone the copies. Even had the word not gotten out that for some unspecified reason Rostnikov was no longer privileged, the system was painfully slow unless the case had a special red stamp indicating that it was being conducted in conjunction with a KGB investigation. No one talked to Rostnikov about his lowered status. They assumed, he was sure, that he had spoken up once too often or that his Jewish wife had finally proved too great a deficit.

Getting up the stairs in his apartment building was long and difficult with an almost useless left leg, but Rostnikov looked at the daily climb as part of his training program. It was amazing how, if he wanted to do so, he could convert the difficulties of normal Moscow life into advantages. A lack of elevators in the city meant climbing stairs. In long lines at stores, Rostnikov could read his American novels. Without a car, Rostnikov had to take the subway and walk miles each week. Others argued that the hard life of a Muscovite made its inhabitants strong, tough, and hard, while Americans, English, and the French were soft from too much convenience. Why, then, Rostnikov thought, do we not live as long as they do? His thoughts had grown morbid, and his mind was wandering. He did not see the young man coming down the stairway who turned a corner on the third floor and almost collided with him.

Rostnikov staggered back, almost falling, and the boy, large, wearing a black T-shirt and American jeans, hurried past him without apology. Rostnikov, who didn't recognize the boy, reached back with his right hand and clasped his right hand over the boy's shoulder.

"What are you doing, you crazy old fool?" the boy said, trying to wriggle out of the firm grasp. The boy was about seventeen, the same age as the young men in the photograph he had spent more than an hour looking at that day, but this boy was bigger, better fed.

"Who are you?" Rostnikov said, still holding the wall with one hand to keep from being pulled off balance.

"Let me—" the boy began, but Rostnikov dug his hand into the shoulder and lifted the boy up, off the stairs. The face before Rostnikov changed from angry defiance to startled, pale fear.

"Who are you?" Rostnikov repeated.

"My shoulder," the boy squealed.

"You are who?" Rostnikov repeated, not particularly happy with himself and realizing that he might well be taking out on this rude boy his frustration with a system and situation over which the boy had no control.

"Pavel Nuretskov," the boy said.

Rostnikov put him down but still gripped the shoulder. "You are related to the Nuretskovs on the sixth floor?"

"Their nephew," the boy said, trying to remove Rostnikov's hairy fingers from his shoulder with no success.

"You are rude," Rostnikov said. "We are living in rude times."

"Okay," the boy said, giving up on removing the fingers.

"Okay?"

"We are living in rude times," Pavel agreed.

"If you see me again," Rostnikov said softly, "you will say good evening or good morning, comrade."

Rostnikov released the shoulder, and the boy hurried down the stairs, rubbing his shoulder and hissing back, "Only if you can catch me, lame foot."

"You catch more with patience than speed," Rostnikov said softly, knowing even a whisper would carry down the stairway and knowing that the disembodied whisper would be more frightening than a bellow. Rostnikov never shouted. When suspects or superiors shouted, Rostnikov always dropped his voice slightly till they wore down or became quiet so they could hear him. Patience was his primary weapon.

Sarah was home and had a meal on the wooden kitchen table: sour cabbage in vinegar and oil, smoked fish, and brown bread with tea.

Something had gone out of Sarah since Rostnikov's plan to leave Russia had failed. She had put on a few pounds, and her generally serious round and handsome face smiled even less than it had previously. She had lost her job in a music shop and was having trouble finding another, though she was now working a bit for one of her many cousins who sold pots and pans. Rostnikov's salary had been badly strained for almost two months.

"Josef?" he asked, hanging up his jacket and moving to the table. "Did he write?"

"No," she said. "And we can't call. We haven't the money."

"I'll call him tomorrow from Petrovka," Rostnikov said, avoiding her eyes and tearing off a chunk of brown bread. "He's all right."

"He's a soldier," she said with a shrug, sitting with her hands in her lap, watching her husband eat. "I might have a job next week. Katerina knows someone, a manager at the foreign secondhand bookstore on Kachalov Street."

Rostnikov paused, his hand on the way to his mouth with a glass of tepid tea. The prospect of his wife's working for the foreign bookstore lightened his heart for an instant. *What was it the English writer Shakespeare said?* he thought. *"Like lark at break of day arising from the sullen earth." Shakespeare should have been a Russian.*

"That's wonderful," he said, "but—"

The "but" was inevitable, part of the protective response of all Russians even when their prospects were better than those of Sarah Rostnikov. Hope was reasonable, but never expect the hope to be fruitful.

After dinner, Rostnikov lifted his weights for an hour, wearing the torn white shirt with "1983 Moscow Senior Championship" printed on it. He knew Sarah considered his wearing the shirt a childish remnant of his moment of triumph a month earlier when he had won the senior park championship. At the same time, he was sure she did not begrudge him his childishness.

The weightlifting routine was a ritual involving the patient shifting of weights after each exercise, because Rostnikov did not have enough weights to leave them on the bars for each session. Thus, whatever weight and routine he ended a workout with became the first routine of his next workout.

He was just finishing his two-handed curls when the knock came at the door. The windows of the apartment were wide open, and a slight breeze had rippled the curtains occasionally but not altered the heat. Sarah sat across the room, watching something on television, but when Rostnikov looked up at her, he had been sure that she was absorbing nothing she saw on the screen.

His eyes had been on her when the knock came, and she had given a little start of fear.

"There's nothing to worry about," he said as the knock came again. He put down the bar and crossed the room. There was a pause and another knock. The knocks were not loud and demanding, nor were they sly and obsequious. They were not the knocks of timid neighbors or aggressive KGB men.

When he opened the door, Zelach's hand was raised, unsure of whether to knock again. His broad and not bright face looked relieved to see Rostnikov before him, sweating, hair plastered down on his forehead.

"I didn't mean to—"

"Come in, Zelach," he said, stepping back.

"This is my wife, Sarah," he said, nodding toward her.

Zelach smiled painfully.

"Tea?" she said.

"I—"

"You may have tea, Zelach, while you tell me why you are here," Rostnikov said, returning to his workout.

"I—"

"And you may sit."

Zelach looked around for someplace to sit, pulled out a kitchen chair, and sat straight and awkward.

"You have something to tell me, or is this simply your first social call?" Rostnikov asked, wiping his wet forehead with his sleeve as he finished his curls. Sarah handed Zelach a cup of tea.

"The photograph," he said. "I made the calls. There is an old woman in Yekteraslav who remembers Savitskaya. I called the district police. My cousin's wife's brother is a sergeant. He went to the village and called me back."

"Why didn't you just call us?" Sarah said politely.

"I was working late," Zelach said. "Inspector Rostnikov said—"

"I appreciate your conscientiousness, Zelach," Rostnikov said, wiping his forehead with his sleeve and moving forward to pat the man's shoulder. Zelach smiled and gulped down his tea. "Tomorrow you and I will take a journey to Yekteraslav on the *electrichka*. We'll take sandwiches and talk to old ladies. Perhaps we'll wander in the fields of wheat."

Zelach looked puzzled.

"They grow soybeans in that area now. My cousin's—"

"Poetry eludes you, Zelach. Did you know that?" Rostnikov said.

"I know," Zelach said. "I was always better in numbers in school, though I was none too good in that."

"Go home now," Rostnikov said, leading Zelach to the door. "You've done well."

Zelach smiled and looked around for someplace to put his empty teacup now that he was half a dozen feet from the table. Rostnikov took it with a nod and ushered the man out the door, giving Zelach just enough time to say a polite good-bye to Sarah.

When the door was closed, he turned to his wife.

"Is it important?" she said with a touch of curiosity he wanted to catch, nurture, and use.

"An old man was murdered this morning," he said. "An old Jewish man."

"And someone cares?" she said with what might have been sarcasm, a mode Rostnikov had seldom seen in his wife.

"I care," said Rostnikov softly, though in truth it was less that he cared about the gnarled old man than about the man's children, especially the woman with the bad leg and the edge of madness to her eyes. And, in truth, it was a case. Somewhere there was a man or woman, men or women, who had committed a crime. The crime had been handed to Rostnikov, and his skill was being challenged by the criminal, possibly by the procurator, and certainly by himself.

"I care," he repeated, and moved toward the bedroom and the shower stall beyond, which he hoped would deliver warm water but from which he expected only a cool dip.

After Vera Shepovik had fired her rifle from the roof of the Ukraine Hotel, she had not wept. She had sobbed in frustration when the gun had jammed after the first shot. Vera's plan had been to kill as many people as possible in case she was caught. She had seen the porter come through the door, weaving slightly, and had backed into the shadows, away from the edge, behind a stone turret. She had wept again in frustration, because she wanted desperately to shoot the obviously drunken little man. For a moment she even considered leaping from behind the protective bricks, beating the man to death with her rifle, and throwing him down to the street. It would have been a minor inconvenience. Vera was a robust woman, a muscular woman who at the age of forty had been an athlete, skilled at both the javelin and hammer. In 1964, she had just missed the Olympic team. That had been the highlight of her life. The lows had been far more plentiful.

First Stefan had been killed. They had told her it was an accident, but it had been no accident. It had been the first step in the conspiracy against her, a conspiracy by the state, the KGB, the police. She knew the reason, too. The steroids. They had urged her to take those steroids for competition and to prepare her for the Olympics. Now, even twenty years later, they were still warning her to keep her quiet, to keep her from from creating an international scandal that might ruin the reputation of the Soviet athletic system. They had, of course, lied to her. One doctor had said she needed psychiatric help, but it was not a psychiatrist she needed; besides, the state didn't believe in psychoanalysis.

No, there was no one to trust. First it had been Stefan they had pushed in front of the metro at the Kurskaya station. Then her father had been murdered. They had said it was a heart attack, that he was seventy-eight years old, drank too much, smoked too much, but she knew the truth. One by one, as a warning to her, they had murdered people she knew. Sometimes they were very subtle. Nikolai Repin, whom she had gone to school with, was dead of some unknown cause. She was told this by another old acquaintance she happened to meet in front of the National Restaurant on Gorky Street. Vera had not seen Nikolai for at least ten years, but this woman, whose name she could not recall, had happened to meet her, had happened to mention his death. Vera was no fool. The meeting had not been by chance. It had been planned, another warning. She had been careful, so careful not to let them know, not to let her mother know of the conspiracy around her. Vera knew they were trying to poison the air in her small apartment, and so for years she had set up a tent in her room, a tent of blankets held up by chairs and the kitchen table. There was ample air under the blanket for the night, though there was always the slight smell of poison in the room each morning, and in the summer it had been almost unbearably hot under the blanket. Her mother had survived miraculously, probably because she had grown immune to the poison. Luck.

Vera had checked her food carefully for years, feeding a bit to Gorki, her cat, before she ate it. She never ate out where they could slip something in.

And then they had gotten through her defenses. Vera wasn't sure how they had done it, probably through special rays in the wall. It didn't matter. They had done it. For almost a year she had kept quiet about the pains in her stomach. Once in a hospital, she was sure they would simply cut her open, remove the remnants of the steroids, and let her die, stomach open, no one caring. They would stuff a rag in her mouth and wheel her into the corner to die, possibly shunt her body into a little closet. They didn't care. She had no use, no value. Then they had finally gotten her into a hospital when she collapsed at the box factory where she worked. The doctor who examined her said Vera had stomach cancer. Vera did not weep. No one would see her weep. They all looked at her with curiosity, as if she were some specimen, some experiment that had gone wrong and now would not quietly die so she could be swept into the garbage.

The doctor had recommended surgery, but Vera had declined. The doctor had not seemed to care. No one seemed to care about Vera. As far as they were concerned, she was already dead, taken care of, gone, swept into the garbage. But they were wrong. They had killed her, but they had made the mistake of not finishing the job.

The Moisin rifle had been her father's in the war. It was too large, too awkward, and she wasn't sure the rifle would work. The bullets were so old. Her father had sometimes taken her hunting when she was a child, and she had been a natural shooter. The idea was simple. She would pay them back, make them realize what they had done. Those people who walked past her, unsmiling, uncaring. She had become a pawn of the state and then had been cast out, and they had been reasonable, all of them who walked past and didn't care what the old men who ran the country did to innocent people like Vera. If she could, she would put a bullet into every solid Soviet face in Moscow, but what she wanted most was to destroy the authorities who conspired against her—police, KGB, the military.

She wept with fury each time she climbed a hotel roof, her rifle hidden in that idiotic trombone case. She had avoided elevators and made the painful trek upward through stairways, fire escapes. And then the rifle, the damned rifle, always had something wrong with it. She had now shot five people. That she knew, but she had no idea of whether she had killed them or not. The newspapers never carried stories on such things. But she knew she had hit them. She had watched them go down. She wanted them dead. They had expected her to be dead in a few months, but it was they who had died first. Each shot was justice.

She could have leaped out that night and killed the porter, but she could not count on her stomach to allow her to make the run. In addition, had she thrown him to the street, someone below might have realized where the shots originated, and the police might come after her, catch her before she was finished.

"What are you doing, Verochka?" her mother called across the room. The old woman was embroidering near the window to catch the sun before it was gone.

Vera had told her mother nothing of the cancer, nothing of her frustration, her anger, her fear.

"Thinking," Vera said.

"Thinking," her mother repeated.

The two were a contrast. The mother, a small round creature with scraggly white hair and thick glasses, the daughter, massive, with a severe pink face and brown hair tied back with hairpins. Vera was more like her father, at least her father when he had been younger.

"Thinking about people," Vera said.

Her mother shrugged, not wanting to pursue the thoughts of the daughter she had long ago given up as mad. There was no resource, no treatment, for the mad in Moscow other than to lock them up. Vera could still work, though she had begun to look pale and had talked less and less each day. Adriana Shepovik was well aware of her daughter's obsession with the old rifle, but she didn't question it. The thing certainly didn't work. The girl had probably been trying from time to time to sell the gun, though Adriana doubted if anyone would buy the piece of junk.

"I'm going out," Vera said, suddenly getting up.

"Eat something."

"I'll eat when I get back," Vera said, reaching down to pet Gorki, who had rubbed against her leg.

Vera went to the closet near the door and reached behind the heavy curtain for the trombone case. She kept her back to the old woman, though she doubted if the woman could see that far.

"I may be home late," Vera said.

Her mother grunted and plunged the needle into the orange material on her lap.

"Very late," Vera repeated, opening the front door and stepping out.

It was possible, Vera thought, that she might not return all night. She was determined this time not to be impatient. The pain in her stomach was growing each day, and the medicine she had been given had helped less and less. The day might come soon when Vera would not be able to go out, climb to the roofs of Moscow, and find justice.

No, tonight she would wait patiently even if it took till dawn. She would wait until she could get a good shot at a policeman.

The *electrichka* had been fast and not particularly crowded. It had been an off hour for travel, around ten when Rostnikov and Zelach left. The ride to Yekteraslav took about an hour, during which Zelach tried to carry on a conversation while Rostnikov grunted and attempted to read his Ed McBain book.

There was no stop at Yekteraslav. They had to get off at Sdminkov. When they left the train, Rostnikov's left leg was almost totally numb. A taxi stood near the station, and Rostnikov limped toward it, with Zelach in front.

"Busy," growled the stubble-faced driver whose curly

gray hair billowed around his face. He did not bother to turn toward the two men.

"Police," said Zelach, getting in and sliding over.

"I'm still—" the driver said wearily, without turning.

Rostnikov reached over after he got in and put his hand on the driver's shoulder.

"What is your name?"

The man winced in pain and turned to face his two passengers. Fear appeared in his eyes.

"I—I thought you were lying," the man said, the smell of fish on his breath. "Smart city people say they are everything to get a cab. I'm supposed to wait here each day for Comrade—"

"Yekteraslav," Rostnikov said, releasing the man so he could massage his shoulder.

"But I—" the man protested.

Rostnikov was already leaning back in the uncomfortable seat with his eyes closed. He would massage his leg as soon as the man started.

"Yekteraslav," Zelach repeated, looking out the window.

The driver looked at his two passengers in the mirror and decided against argument.

Fifteen minutes later, after rumbling over a stone road in need of repair, the driver grumbled, "Yekteraslav."

Rostnikov opened his eyes and looked out the window at a looming three-story factory belching smoke on the town's thirty or forty houses and sprinkling of isbas, the old wooden houses without toilets.

"Where?" the driver said.

"Police headquarters," Zelach said.

The driver hurried on.

The bureaucracy of the local police delayed them for half an hour and did little to ease their way to the home of Yuri Pashkov. To say the home was modest would be kind. It was little better than a shack with a small porch on which an ancient man was seated on a wooden chair, watching, as the two heavy policemen ambled forward. The sad-faced younger man deferred to the slightly older man with the bad leg. Yuri was intrigued by the older man, but he showed nothing.

"You are Yuri Pashkov?" Zelach asked.

"I am well aware of who I am," the old man said, looking away at the fascinating spectacle of the factory.

"Would you rather have the conversation at the police station?" Zelach said, stepping onto the porch. Yuri shrugged and looked up at the man.

"You want to carry me to police headquarters, carry me," the old man said.

"Your tongue will get you in trouble," Zelach warned, falling back on the threats of his trade.

"Ha," Yuri cackled. "I'm eighty-five years old. What have you to threaten me with? My family is gone. This shack is a piece of shit. Threaten. Go ahead. Threaten."

Rostnikov stepped up on the small porch into the slight shade from the wooden slats above.

"What kind of factory have you here?" he said.

"Vests."

Rostnikov glanced at the old man in the chair. The lines on his face were amazingly deep and leathery.

"Vests?" Rostnikov asked, sensing the man's favorite subject.

"Vests," the old man said, pausing to spit into the dirt near Zelach, who stepped back. "We used to farm around here, and now they have us working in a factory, and what do we make in that factory?"

"Vests," said Rostnikov.

"Exactly," said Yuri, recognizing a kindred spirit. "What dignity is there in a man's life when he has spent it sewing buttons on vests to be worn by Hungarians or Italians."

"None," Rostnikov agreed.

"None," Yuri said. "And so they make vests without heart, spirit, need. You know what kind of vests they make?"

"Vests of poor quality," Rostnikov guessed, glancing at Zelach, who clearly ached to shake the old rag of a man into a cooperation that would never come.

"Vests of paper, toilet paper, vests not fit to wipe one's ass with," the old man said with venom, spit forming on his mouth, eyes turned always toward the factory.

"It wasn't always like this," Rostnikov said softly.

"There were times," the old man said.

"Long ago," Rostnikov agreed.

"Long ago," Yuri agreed.

"I understand you remember a man named Abraham Savitskaya who was here a long time ago," Rostnikov said, not looking at the man.

"I don't remember."

Zelach stepped forward, whipped the photograph from his pocket, and thrust it in front of the wrinkled face.

"That," said Zelach, "is you. And that is Savitskaya."

"And you are Comrade Shit," the old man said sweetly.

"Zelach," Rostnikov said firmly before the sweating, weary policeman could crush the dry old man. "Walk back to the police station, arrange for a car to get us to the station in time to catch the next train."

Zelach's face displayed a rush of thought: first the consideration of defiance, and then its quick suppression, followed by petulance, and finally resignation.

When Zelach had gone, Rostnikov leaned against the wall and said no. "What happened to your leg?"

"Battle of Rostov," Yuri said. "I still have poison gas in my lungs. I can taste it when I belch."

They watched the factory a while longer before the old man spoke again.

"Some didn't stay around to face the troubles, the Germans, the Revolution."

"Some?" Rostnikov tried gently.

"Savitskaya," he said. "Savitskaya and Mikhail."

"Mikhail?"

"Mikhail Posniky," the old man said. "After the first Revolution, they fled."

"Mikhail Posniky is the third man in the photograph?"

Yuri shrugged, the closest he would come to cooperation.

"What happened to him?"

"They left, said they were going to America. Who knows? We were supposed to be friends, but they ran like cowards."

"They should have stayed," Rostnikov agreed.

"To make vests?" said the old man.

"To fight the Nazis," Rostnikov answered.

"Who knew in 1920 the Nazis were coming?" the old man said, looking at his feebleminded police guest.

"Who knew?" Rostnikov agreed. "And the fourth man?"

Pashkov shrugged and shivered. "I don't know."

Rostnikov was sure, however, that the man did know. His face had paled, and he had folded his hands on his lap. His arthritic fingers had held each other to keep from trembling.

"You are Jewish," Rostnikov said.

"Ah," Yuri said, laughing. "I knew it was coming. It always comes. I fought. This village fought. And you people come and—"

"The four of you were Jewish?" Rostnikov said, stepping in front of the old man and cutting off his view of the factory.

"Some of us still are," Pashkov said defiantly. "Those of us who are alive, at least one, me." He pointed a gnarled finger at his own chest.

"The fourth man," Rostnikov repeated. *"Who is he?"*

"I forget," Pashkov said, showing yellow teeth barely rooted to his gums.

"You forget nothing," Rostnikov said, looking down.

"I forget what I must forget. I'm a very old man."

"A name," Rostnikov said, and then softly added, "My wife is Jewish."

"You lie, comrade policeman," the old man said.

Rostnikov reached into his back pocket with a grunt, removed his wallet, and fished through it till he found the picture of Sarah and his identification papers. He handed them to the old man.

"You could have prepared these just to fool me," he

said, handing the photograph and papers back to the man who blocked his view of the loved and hated factory.

"I could have," Rostnikov agreed. "But I didn't, and you know I didn't."

"I know," Pashkov said, painfully rising, using the side of the house to help him to a level of near dignity. "He was not a pleasant boy."

"And you are afraid?"

"Vests," Yuri Pashkov spat, coming to a decision. "His name was Shmuel Prensky. Beyond that I know nothing. He cooperated with the Stalinist pishers who came here in, I don't know, 1930, '31. He helped them. . . .I have nothing more to say."

"You were afraid of him?" Rostnikov said, stepping out of the man's line of sight.

"I'm still afraid of him," Yuri whispered. "May you carry my damnation for bringing his name and memory back to me, for reminding me of those dark eyes that betrayed his own people. I damn you for bringing that photograph."

Rostnikov stepped back and let the trembling man return to his chair and to his thoughts of useless vests and distant Italians wearing them.

There was nothing more to say. Rostnikov had two names now, and if Sofiya Savitskaya was right in her identification, the name of the killer of her father was Mikhail Posniky.

"The other man in the photograph, the fifth man," Rostnikov tried, hoping to catch the old man before he was completely lost. "The little man."

"Lev, Lev Ostrovsky," Yuri answered, sighing. "The clown, the actor."

"Actor?"

"He stayed through the troubles and moved to Moscow." The word Moscow came out like the spit of a dry, dirty word. "He left to become an actor. His father had been the rabbi here. But we had no need for rabbis or the sons of rabbis when Shmuel Prensky and his friends . . ."

He never finished the sentence. His eyes closed and

then his mouth, hiding what little remained of lips. The sun was hot and high, and Rostnikov was tired and hungry. The walk to the police station was far and dry, but Porfiry Petrovich did not mind. He had some names to work with. He wanted to hurry back to Moscow, for it was there a survivor existed who might provide a link in the puzzle of the murder of Abraham Savitskaya.

FOUR

THE YOUNG MAN AND WOMAN WALKED ALONG GRANovsky Street arm in arm. People who passed them in the late afternoon assumed the man had obtained his flattened nose in some hockey or soccer game. He was burly, rugged looking, and his straight black hair, falling over his forehead, bounced athletically as he moved. He talked easily and loudly. He wore a clean blue short-sleeved shirt that revealed his well-developed biceps and added to his image as an athlete. It was also appropriate that the woman with him was quite beautiful and strikingly blond, her hair worn back in an American-style ponytail. She was not thin like an American, however. She was full and athletic appearing, possibly weighing about 140 pounds and looking as if she had just rolled up her sleeves and stepped out of a poster for increasing production in the steel industry. All she needed was a flag. She wore no makeup, and needed none. Health beamed from their faces, and Vera Shepovik glanced at them as she passed, cursed them silently, and wished that she could cross to the park, get out her father's old rifle, and burn the joy of life from their faces.

Vera, however, was a half mile away when the couple passed in front of a large apartment building, one of the many on the street that housed the most important and privileged *nachalstvo*, bosses, in the Soviet Union. A chauffeur-driven car stood in front of one building where Chernenko supposedly lived. The couple paid no attention but whispered something to each other that the driver, pretending to look straight ahead, assumed was sexual. It made the driver shift and wish he could remove the jacket of his semimilitary uniform. It was a hot day, a muggy hot Thursday.

A jogger, complete with Western sweat suit, flew past the young couple, seriously intent on three or four miles before dinner. His hair was white, and he was lean and fit, an unusual figure on the streets of Moscow. The serious joggers were like this one, head forward, arms low, pace steady. The less serious moved slowly, sometimes almost walking. The jogging suit made it clear, the runner hoped, that he was indeed running and not simply walking.

As the couple passed a group of men and women arriving home from work, the woman tugged at the sleeve of the young man and pointed at a white Chaika parked in front of an apartment building about four car lengths from the building's entrance. He seemed at first reluctant to look at the car but then smiled weakly and gave in. Like two honeymooners, they peered through the window and examined the upholstery of the car that the likes of them would never own.

"Well," said the man in a pebbly voice from a throat planed dry by too much vodka.

The woman smiled, her pink cheeks a contrast to the broken veins on the man's nose, visible at close range.

"Yes," she said decisively.

The street was relatively clear. Cars passed, the sound of traffic rattled past them, and pedestrians ambled forward, carrying cloth shopping bags and briefcases. Standing on the sidewalk, his eyes toward the front of the apartment building, the muscular man, who looked not quite so young at close range, leaned against the car as the woman moved to his side to join him. Behind her back she tried to open the door to the Chaika. It was locked. They talked of this and that and nothing for a few seconds, mentioned a possible picnic in the park, and waited for a break in the crowd. It came, a brief one, and the woman turned, pulling a hollow metal tube of twelve inches or so from her bag. Quickly, without looking back, she leaned forward and thrust the steel tube against the car's window. Her arms were strong and the thrust powerful. The bar penetrated the window almost noiselessly and the circle of glass fell to the plush seat within. She withdrew the bar to the patter of the man with the mashed nose, who repeated, "*Khorosho*, good" as she worked. She dropped the bar into her shopping bag, pushed her fingers through the small hole, and lifted the button inside.

She stood, turned again, and looked around the street. They continued to look like a pair of lovers who had paused on their nightly walk to admire the apartments of the great and near-great men who ran the country.

"Now," she said softly when an older couple passed in front of them. Had the older couple paid more attention to the two at the car, they would have seen that the man was perspiring. The sun was already going down, and the early evening was turning cool.

The young woman turned, opened the door of the white car, slid across the seat, and pulled a metal bar and a wire with a clip at the end of her shopping bag as the man jumped in at her side, closed the door, and looked back over his shoulder.

"Use the mirror," the woman said without looking up from what she was doing under the dashboard. "Don't draw attention."

The man wiped his forehead and glanced at the mirror without looking at the woman. He tried to keep himself from panting like a dog as he counted slowly. By the time he reached seven, the woman had started the car. He stopped counting as she sat up. In the rearview mirror, he saw a pair of men step out of the apartment building and look around. They glanced at the Chaika, and the young man reached inside his jacket for the pistol, which stuck clammily to his stomach.

"Go," he said. "Go."

She sat up with maddening calm, looked back over her shoulder for an opening in traffic, and began to ease out of the space. In the mirror, the man saw the two men at the apartment entrance turn the other way and wave.

"Done, Ilya," the woman said. He looked at her beautiful, strong face and marveled once again at her coolness. Ilya wanted nothing more than a drink.

"When we get this to the garage, we are done, Marina," he said, opening the glove compartment to keep his hands from trembling.

As Marina sped along Botanical Street past Dzerzhinsky Recreation Park, a dog shot into the street. She swerved deftly to miss it and barely avoided a collision with a tourist bus. Oriental faces peered out the bus window.

"Drive carefully," Ilya hissed between closed teeth.

"Next time I'll hit the dog," she said jokingly.

It was then that he found the report among the papers in the glove compartment and almost threw up on the freshly scented seat of the newly shampooed Chaika. He controlled the hot, vile, small ball of fear that rose from his stomach to his throat and spoke as calmly as he could, which, he was sure, was not calm at all.

"This car belongs to the deputy procurator general at Moscow," he said, almost in a whisper.

"No," Marina replied calmly, looking out of the window, her arm on the open window as she glided along like a movie star. "It belongs to us."

The train ride back from Yekteraslav was hell. Zelach brooded, pouted, almost sucked his thumb. He shifted and squirmed and demanded more attention than a petulant child. Rostnikov's leg hurt at the knee, and he couldn't read. He knew he would have to face Sarah's growing anguish if she hadn't found work. He worried about Josef, his son, and wondered why there had been no letters from him in Kiev for almost three weeks. Rostnikov tried to build a tale from the bits of information he had gathered about the old men in the photograph. Nothing came. He put the book aside and turned to Zelach.

"Why the brass candlestick?" he said.

Zelach shrugged.

"Hidden value? An antique?" Rostnikov went on as the train rattled forward, buzzing electrically. There were few passengers going toward the city in the late afternoon. Passengers were going the other way, away from Moscow as the workday ended. It had not been difficult to catch a train. They ran frequently, a tribute to the efficiency of the system, according to Emil Karpo. Rostnikov had once suggested to Karpo in return that it demonstrated quite the reverse. Because the train system had to meet its quota of hours in service, trains often ran empty, sometimes in the middle of the night, wasting power. They were ghosts, zombies plodding forward to meet quotas like the vest factory in Yekteraslav. Rostnikov had discovered that the vest factory often went twenty-four hours in ceaseless production of second-rate vests for which there was no market. Work quotas had to be met. People had to be kept busy.

"It may have been incriminating," Rostnikov went on.

"What?" Zelach answered drowsily.

"The brass candlestick the killers took from the Savitskaya's apartment."

Zelach shrugged. The candlestick held no interest for him. His impulse toward enthusiasm had waned with the afternoon. Zelach was exhausted from two days of effort to impress the Washtub. The trip and that leathery old man had proved too much for Zelach. A conductor came past to check tickets, and Zelach scowled at him. Zelach would gladly have paid his own way back to that town for the joy of crushing the skull of that old man on the porch who had led to Zelach's humiliation.

"Fifty years, more than fifty years, can you imagine that?" Rostnikov said, folding his hands on his lap over the American novel. "Perhaps the very year I was born, maybe even before, these young men are together in this little village, friends, and then . . . what?"

"What?" said Zelach, not caring what or who or why or when.

Rostnikov turned his face to his subordinate. "Where is your soul, Alexei Stepanovich Zelach?"

"There is no such thing as a soul," Zelach said, trying to hide his irritation.

"Fine," Rostnikov agreed. "Then you have no soul.

Where is your curiosity? What do you think of? What drives you each day, gets you out of bed, into that old suit?"

"I'm not a philosopher," Zelach said uncomfortably.

"I didn't ask for philosophy," Rostnikov sighed. "I was seeking conversation."

"I'm not very good at talking, chief inspector. You are well aware of that."

Rostnikov considered returning to his book, but he knew Zelach would find some way to gain his attention. Rostnikov had made up his mind. He would find some diversion for Zelach, something to keep the man busy and, he hoped, useful, something to keep him as distant as possible while Rostnikov worked on the murder of Abraham Savitskaya.

"Are we working tonight?" Zelach said, looking out the window at the first tall buildings that indicated they were approaching Moscow. "I'll get some sandwiches and bring them to the office."

"No," said Rostnikov. "Go home. In the morning I will have a new assignment for you."

Zelach grunted and looked out the window at the familiar surroundings of Moscow.

It was almost seven in the evening when Rostnikov got to Petrovka Street. He had fought the crowds with success and emerged a bit weary from the Sverdlov Square metro station. The sun was almost down and the evening not quite so hot as he crossed the square, went through the park, around the Karl Marx monument, and waited patiently for the traffic to slow so he could limp across Marx Prospekt and move past the shadow of the massive USSR State Academic Bolshoi Theatre.

Minutes later he stepped into Petrovka, the twin ten-story buildings that house the police operations of the city of Moscow. The buildings are modern, utilitarian, and always busy. The people of Moscow know where to find Petrovka, for it is not hidden, nor are the thousands of gray-clad policemen who patrol the city. Indeed, the ratio of police to populace is higher in Moscow than in any other major city of the world.

In spite of this, crime, while it does not flourish, exists. Files of *poznaniye*, or inquiries, cover the desks of the procurators working under the procurator general of the Soviet Union. The police work with the procurators in the twenty districts of Moscow and are responsible for all but political crimes. Political crimes fall within the sphere of the KGB (Komitet Gosudarstvennoi Beszopasnosti,) or State Security Agency. It was a constant puzzle to Porfiry Petrovich Rostnikov what a political crime might be. Economic crimes are generally political, because they threaten the economy of the state and are subversive. In fact, however, Rostnikov knew that any crime could be considered political, even the beating of a wife by a drunken husband. Officially, the procurator general's office is empowered by the constitution (Fundamental Law) of the Union of Soviet Socialist Republics, adapted at the Seventh (Special) Session of the Supreme Soviet of the USSR, Ninth Convocation, on October 7, 1977, according to Article 164, to exercise "supreme power of supervision over the strict and uniform observance of laws by all ministries, state committees and departments, enterprises, institutions and organizations, executive-administrative bodies of local Soviets of People's Deputies, collective farms, cooperatives, and other public organizations, officials, and citizens."

When he entered the station, Rostnikov planned to head for his small office on the fifth floor, pick up any messages, take care of them, sit quietly in the solitude of his only place of refuge outside the toilet in his apartment, and rest for an hour or two before going home. He planned, of course, to call his wife and give her a half lie about his tardiness, but it would only be a half lie if there was no work to do. He would spend the time doodling on the sheets of rough paper and thinking about the old Jewish man in the bathtub and his daughter, this frightened daughter with the leg as stiff as his own.

However, he did not get to his office right away. As he

entered the building, the uniformed officer at the desk, behind whom stood another uniformed officer with a ready Sten gun, called to Rostnikov.

"Inspector," the man called. "The assistant procurator wants you to come to his office the moment you arrive."

Rostnikov nodded and made his way to the elevator. It was late for the deputy procurator still to be in. The former deputy, Anna Timofeyeva, had spent as much as eighteen hours a day working until her heart attacks had sent her into retirement in a one-room apartment shared by her cat, Bakunin.

Like former procurator Timofeyeva, Procurator Khabolov had no training in law. Anna Timofeyeva had been the assistant to one of the commissars of Leningrad in charge of shipping and manufacturing quotas. A zealot, she had learned the job of procurator well and with reasonable intelligence had done as well as anyone to combat crime. Khabolov, on the other hand, had come to his first ten-year term as a deputy procurator after having made a name for himself as a trouble-shooter who ferreted out slacking and shirking among factory workers. It was the hound-dog-faced Khabolov who had discovered the tunnel in the piston factory in Odessa, the tunnel through which workers were smuggling vodka, which they consumed in large quantities, leading to the slowdown of production and the failure to meet quotas. Comrade Khabolov had also, through the payment of strategic bribes, discovered how a trio of government dock workers had funneled Czech toothpaste into the black market. Suspicion was the primary tool of the new deputy.

Rostnikov made his way to the door of the deputy procurator and knocked. There was no answer for about fifteen seconds, and then the high voice shouted, "Come."

Khabolov sat behind the desk, looking down at the file in front of him, apparently barely aware of Rostnikov. But Rostnikov knew that the man had set the scene, had picked up the file as a prop to prepare himself for the inspector.

"Sit," Khabolov said without looking up.

Rostnikov sat in the wooden chair opposite the deputy

and looked up at the photograph of Lenin left over from the days of Anna Timofeyeva. The photograph had meant much to that box of a woman. Rostnikov was sure that it remained only as another prop for the ambitious dog of a man behind the desk.

Like Anna Timofeyeva, Khabolov also wore his uncomfortable brown uniform, but the button at the neck was undone. To Procurator Timofeyeva, the uniform had been a reminder of her duty. To Khabolov, it was a badge of his authority. That Rostnikov had little respect for the new procurator was evident to both men, but nothing on the inspector's face or in his manner let the fact be known.

Finally, Khabolov made a check mark on the file in front of him and put the file on the stack to his left with the pencil atop it to indicate that he planned only a brief moment or two with Rostnikov before he got back to the more serious business that awaited him.

Rostnikov wanted to shift his stiff leg but did not do so. Instead, he sat, betraying no emotion, and waited.

"The old Jew," Khabolov said. "Are you making progress?"

The game would have to be played out. Khabolov had no interest in the dead Abraham Savitskaya. Whatever was really on his mind would come when he was ready, after he had reminded Rostnikov once again of his demotion, had hinted, once again, at his vulnerability and his Jewish wife.

"I am making progress, comrade procurator," Rostnikov said evenly.

"Good," the procurator said, looking down at his folded hands. Rostnikov, too, looked at the hands. The knuckles were white. Rostnikov had more experience reading people by their actions than did the new deputy procurator. It was quite evident that Khabolov did not want to get on with what he planned.

"Are you aware of what has been happening here today?" Khabolov said. "The various . . . cases."

"No, comrade. I have just returned from Yekteraslav as part of the—"

"My automobile has been stolen," Khabolov's watery

brown eyes rose to meet those of Rostnikov, to challenge them, warn them, search them for the slightest flicker or sign of amusement. Rostnikov displayed nothing.

"I am sorry to hear that, comrade procurator," Rostnikov said.

"I want that car found," Khabolov said. "This ring of car thieves is operating right under our feet. They must be found and finished, quickly and quietly. Do you understand?"

"I understand," Rostnikov said, and he did indeed understand. Khabolov was embarrassed. He could keep the theft quiet for a while, perhaps as long as a week, but eventually it would get out, and he would become a joke, his reputation ruined, his likelihood of advancement stunted.

"Assistant Inspector Tkach has been searching for the enemies of the state who have been stealing automobiles," Khabolov said. "He has made no progress. You are to assist him, to find my Chaika, to find all the cars and to find them quickly."

"And the murder..."

"The murder of an old Jew is not as important as this threat to public confidence," Khabolov said.

"I understand," Rostnikov replied.

"I'm sure you do."

"I'll begin immediately. But comrade, I thought I was not to be assigned to important cases, that I was considered—" Rostnikov began, trying to sound as innocent as possible.

"I'm not a fool, Rostnikov," Khabolov said. "Don't play me for one. We understand each other."

Khabolov had been right. Rostnikov had risked too much, perhaps because he was tired, perhaps because he disliked the man before him so intensely. Rostnikov pushed himself up.

"I've not dismissed you, chief inspector," Khabolov said, and Rostnikov realized that more was coming.

"A police officer has been killed, shot near the Kalinin

Bridge on Kutuzovsky Prospekt," Khabolov said, softly reaching for his file again.

Rostnikov sat again and waited patiently, forcing himself to imagine the three moves it would take to clean and jerk three hundred pounds, forcing himself to cover the urge to shout or reach over and strangle the putrid bureaucrat across from him.

"I'm sorry," Rostnikov said as he was supposed to. "Who . . . ?"

"We do not know who did it," Khabolov responded, pretending to read the file in front of him. "It was probably the sniper we have labeled the Weeper. The shot was apparently fired from the roof of the Ukraine Hotel, as was the shot several days ago."

"I meant who—" Rostnikov tried again.

"Karpo," Khabolov interrupted, savoring the game. "Inspector Karpo is in charge of the case, but he has just come back from a long illness and could use help. I'd like you to supervise that investigation also. We must have results quickly."

"Who was the policeman?" Rostnikov said slowly, almost slowly enough to be considered insolent, but Khabolov had dealt Rostnikov a card that permitted the risk. Khabolov needed the disgraced chief inspector, was admitting that his experience was essential if the deputy procurator was to retain his own job. It was also evident that Khabolov resented this need and hated Rostnikov even more than he had when the morning had begun.

"The officer's name was Petrov," Khabolov said, pursing his lips at the file. "Did you know him?"

"I knew him," Rostnikov said, remembering the freckled, eager face of Sergeant Petrov; the cold day almost a year earlier when Petrov had volunteered to enter a state liquor store in which three frightened and armed teenagers were trapped; Petrov's rush across the open space of the narrow street, steam coming from his mouth.

"I knew him," Rostnikov repeated.

"I heard you the first time, comrade," Khabolov said.

"We can't let lunatics shoot our officers on the street in broad daylight."

"Yes, nighttime would be much better," Rostnikov agreed.

"Inspector," Khabolov said, putting the file down slowly, deliberately. "Let us understand each other."

"I am sure we do, comrade procurator. I will talk to Inspector Karpo immediately and make the investigation of the sniper murders our number-one priority."

"Wait," Khabolov said, rising as Rostnikov limped toward the door. "I don't want those automobile thieves lost sight of."

Rostnikov turned to the man behind the desk, blinked once, and said, "Then auto thieves have priority over the killer of a police officer?"

The answer was evident to both men. Of course, the auto thief was more important. The deputy procurator's reputation was at stake. The killer of policemen was high priority indeed, but nothing compared to a reputation.

"I understand," Rostnikov said before Khabolov could form an answer. He closed the door gently behind him and listened. He thought he caught the sigh of a single word from the new deputy procurator. *Koshmar*, the sigh came, nightmare.

As he moved slowly down the stairs, Rostnikov felt two conflicting urges. The first was a sense of joy, joy at the prospect of new power, the prospect of Khabolov's humiliation, but the joy faded before it could truly form as he remembered the freckled face of Sergeant Petrov.

FIVE

SINCE SERGEANT PETROV WAS A POLICE OFFICER, A member of the military police and not the procuracy, Colonel Snitkonoy, the Gray Wolfhound, had to be dealt with. Colonel Snitkonoy was outraged, incensed, furious, and prepared to fuss and fume for hours if need be until serious attention was paid to him.

There was a time, Rostnikov knew, when the colonel had indeed been a wolfhound, had pursued criminals with vengeance in his heart and blood on his teeth. The Gray Wolfhound was a marked contrast to Porfiry the Washtub, his counterpart. Snitkonoy was tall, with distinguished gray temples, slender but not thin, the sculpted features of a Rublev painting. He was impressive, never a line askew on his bemedaled uniform. Even the medals were lean and orchestrated, not a double line of cartoon festoonery but a discrete trio of ribbons chosen for their color rather than their import.

The Gray Wolfhound was indeed impressive, but he had become essentially hollow. The administration of the military police had changed around him; it had, in the course of fifteen years, become more bureaucratic and, in some ways, more efficient. Snitkonoy looked like, and was, a remnant of a past era. The chiseled Sherlockian profile now seemed almost comic, and Snitkonoy found himself being used increasingly as a figurehead for public gatherings, an actor to be presented to visiting dignitaries.

Foreign visitors, at least those not experienced at such

deception, left Moscow, after having met Snitkonoy, convinced that they had experienced the rare privilege of an audience with a great and busy man. One enchanted Bulgarian had even gone back to Sofia and penned a novel using a distinctly Snitkonoy-like figure as the protagonist.

Porfiry Petrovich sat quietly, hands folded on the conference-room table, and listened to the Gray Wolfhound. It was still early on Friday morning, though Rostnikov had already met with Zelach, Karpo, and Tkach briefly in his own small office. He had assigned Zelach to a new task that would keep him out of the way, had impressed Tkach with the importance of finding Comrade Khabolov's Chaika, and had offered his assistance to Emil Karpo, who had indicated that he would do whatever the procurator thought best in the case of the weeping sniper. Rostnikov's stomach had rumbled, bringing a nervous laugh from Zelach. It had been the only moment of levity in the brief meeting before Porfiry Petrovich and Karpo had to attend the meeting in the conference room in the second tower of Petrovka.

"The resources of the entire militia will be mobilized for this effort," the Wolfhound said, striking his palm against the polished table for emphasis. Rostnikov had already lifted his cup from the table in anticipation of the gesture. He had been to other conferences hosted by the Wolfhound, and he knew it was coming. Karpo, at his side, had no tea, and most of the others in the room, five of them, had also been to conferences with the most famous member of the military police. Only one drowsy newly appointed man of about fifty with a pink face and round cheeks was taken in by the performance. His full cup of tea tottered and overflowed. The pink man leaned over to wipe the table with his sleeve.

Porfiry Petrovich leaned over to make a note on his pad of ragged paper, a move that pleased Snitkonoy. The note read, "The entire militia running around on Gorky Street, bumping into each other, possibly killing more people than the Weeper." He drew two stick figures of uniformed policemen bumping into each other and then he crossed them out. The image of Petrov's face began to form on the paper. Rostnikov sighed and found himself drawing a candlestick.

"Questions?" the Wolfhound said, folding his arms and looking around the table.

"What, precisely, is the militia doing?" asked the newcomer with the pink face.

The proper question, Rostnikov thought, was "What are we wasting our time here for?"

The Gray Wolfhound smirked knowingly, as if the pink-faced man's question was the one he expected. He turned to the map of Moscow behind him on the wall and began to point to buildings as he spoke.

"For the next three weeks an armed officer will be placed atop the Ukraine Hotel, the Council for Mutual Economic Assistance Building, the Mir Hotel on Kalinin Prospekt, the Moskva Hotel on Sverdlov Square, the *Izvestia* building on Gorky Street, all the buildings from which it is believed the Weeper has fired. This, on the assumption that he will return to one of them as he has apparently returned to the Ukraine Hotel. Further questions?"

"Did Sergeant Petrov have a family?" Rostnikov asked, looking up from his doodles.

"I don't know," said the Wolfhound, rubbing his palms together. "How is that relevant?"

Instead of answering, Rostnikov merely shrugged. The Gray Wolfhound was not someone he had to appease.

"We will catch our sniper within the week, two weeks at the latest," Snitkonoy said, right palm to his chest. "This I personally promise."

"We are reassured," said Rostnikov, putting the finishing touches to the cube he was shading in. Snitkonoy has made such promises before. On one or two occasions, he had actually succeeded in keeping the promise, though the success had little to do with the colonel.

"We've talked enough," Snitkonoy said, glancing at Rostnikov, whom he clearly could not fathom. "Comrades, it's time to work."

The pink man rose and then looked around in embarrassment when no one else moved. He sat down quickly as everyone else in the room except for Karpo and Rostnikov got up. The others had expected Snitkonoy to try to hold on to his audience, but possibly the disturbing presence of the Washtub had dissuaded him. The Wolfhound was the first out of the room. His gait had been martial, determined, as if he were on the way to do personal battle with the Weeper. In fact, as everyone but the pink man knew, the Wolfhound would head back to his office to wait until he was needed to perform another ceremonial public act.

When the room had cleared, the pink man stood and addressed Rostnikov and Karpo.

"We have not been introduced, comrades. I am Sergei Yefros of the Soviet Afro-Asian Solidarity Committee."

And what, thought Rostnikov, *are you doing at this meeting?*

"I don't know why I was told to come to this meeting," the pink-faced little man said apologetically in answer to the unstated but obvious question. "I think there may have been some mistake."

"Impossible," said Rostnikov sternly. "We don't make mistakes. Colonel Snitkonoy makes no mistakes."

"No," the man said, shuffling sideways toward the door and pointing to his own chest with his open palm. "I meant I made a mistake. I . . . made . . . I made a mistake. Do you see?"

"That," Rostnikov conceded, "is possible." And the man plunged through the door, leaving Rostnikov and Karpo alone in the room. For a full minute the two men sat in silence, Rostnikov with his lips pursed, looking for the answer to a murder in the crude candlestick he had drawn; Karpo trying to think of nothing—and almost succeeding.

"Two questions, Comrade Karpo," Rostnikov said with a sigh. "First, why would someone murder an old man and take only a brass candlestick."

Karpo did not for an instant consider that Rostnikov's question might be a joke. Karpo had no sense of what a joke might be. He knew that other people engaged in non sequiturs, incongruities, insults, physical misdemeanors, at which they laughed or smiled. He had never understood the process or function of comedy. And so he answered where others might have been wary.

"It is unlikely that the murder was committed for the candlestick," Karpo said, looking straight ahead, "but that you know."

Rostnikov nodded and kept drawing.

"Was the candlestick new, old, very old?"

"Very old," Rostnikov said. "Perhaps a hundred years or more, but probably not an antique of any value, certainly not enough value for a well-dressed foreigner to covet."

"Then," concluded Karpo, "it could have been a trick, a ploy to lead us into thinking that it was important, to send us looking in the wrong direction, which would be very foolish and very clever at the same time."

"Foolish?"

"Because," said Karpo evenly, "we will pursue both the candlestick and the man. We will rely on no assumed link between the two but pursue both. We have the advantage of not tiring."

Rostnikov looked at Karpo and the map of Moscow. Almost eight million people, the fourth largest city in the world, Moscow on the map looked like the cross-section of a log or tree stump, the rings of which tell its age—the Kremlin at the center, around it five rings, each historically marking where the city's boundaries were centuries ago, on which were built wooden palisades, stone walls, and earthen ramparts. In those days it was only possible to enter Moscow through special gates built into the battlements.

The second ring, the Boulevard Ring, is lined with trees and is a band of lush green in the summer. The third ring, the Garden Ring, is the transport artery, sixteen kilometers around the center of the city. Farther out is the fourth ring, which two centuries ago served as the city's customs boundary and on which now runs the Moscow Circular Railway. Finally, the fifth ring, a modern ring, the Moscow Circular Motor Road, marks the city's present boundary.

"I get very tired, comrade," Rostnikov said.

"Individually, yes," Karpo responded seriously. "But we are not individuals alone. We are part of a determined whole."

"Which," said Rostnikov, putting his pencil down and turning awkwardly to face his pale subordinate, "brings me to my second question. When will you admit that your arm is no longer capable of function? When will you let it be examined by a competent doctor?"

As long as Karpo had known Rostnikov, almost fifteen years, he had frequently been lulled by the man's manner into making mistakes. Karpo vowed to himself each time to be more careful, but he also took pride in his superior's ability to penetrate, to trick sympathetically. If the individual was not so important, why did Karpo not admit his handicap and step down for a more able investigator? Was not the loss of the use of an arm sufficient cause to step down, to recognize that there could well be situations with which one could not cope?

"Perhaps never," Karpo said, unblinking eyes fixed on his superior.

Rostnikov rose with a sigh, holding the table with his right hand till he could straighten his left leg under him.

"Never?"

"When I catch the Weeper, perhaps," Karpo amended. The amendment was necessary. Karpo lived by reason and dedication. It was only reasonable to come to this conclusion.

"You don't have to retire even if you discover you have one arm," Rostnikov said, shaking his head. "I have, in effect, only one leg, and the Gray Wolfhound has but half a brain."

"I do not wish to be a detriment to—"

"Ha," Rostnikov interrupted in mock exasperation. "With one arm you are the best man in the procuracy. See, now you have forced me to embarrass both you and myself by extending flattery. You keep on like this, and I will soon be cordial, then polite, and we will find ourselves in a situation in which we are like that pink panda who just shambled out of here."

Karpo rose and nodded in agreement. "I will take your suggestion under advisement," Karpo said.

"The Weeper," Rostnikov said, holding back a morning yawn.

"The Weeper may return to any of those hotel roofs," Karpo said softly.

"He appears to be a creature of habit," Rostnikov prodded.

Karpo nodded and went on. "The attacks are coming more frequently. I believe the Weeper is on some time schedule, some constraint. I believe the Weeper is no longer shooting randomly but that Sergeant Petrov was an intended victim. I've examined the reports of the incidents, spoke to those who were nearby. For every attack there was at least one nearby witness in uniform, military or police. The Weeper has simply grown confident or angry enough to fire at the real intended victims."

"And you conclude from this?" Rostnikov said with a small smile.

"That another attack will take place soon where people in uniform can be readily found."

"That could be—"

"Many places," said Karpo. "I am well aware of that. I would like to post men who would be well hidden atop the high buildings facing military establishments within Moscow and perhaps a man atop the Destky Mir children's shop across from KGB headquarters. And, of course, atop this building."

Rostnikov pocketed his doodles, shook his head, and smiled. "You have no evidence," he said. "This is all concoction."

"I remind the chief inspector that in the past I—"

"—have been right about such things," Rostnikov finished. Karpo's statement about his own record had been given without ego. He spoke not out of pride but confidence, a willingness to pursue. He might turn out to be quite wrong, but Rostnikov knew that Karpo would not mind, that he would simply formulate another theory, and another and another, and pursue until he caught the Weeper or someone else did so.

"You will have your men atop buildings, but I cannot take responsibility for placing anyone across from KGB headquarters," Rostnikov said, reaching for the door. "It would be difficult to explain why we have not informed the KGB about our plan if we were caught. No, the KGB will have to rely on its reputation. Besides, they are more expendable than we are. There are so many more of them."

Karpo gave no sign that he recognized irony in the Washtub's words or manner. He simply nodded in agreement and moved to follow Rostnikov out of the now-open door.

"One final thing," the Washtub said. "Why do you think the Weeper might be a woman?"

"I didn't say—" Karpo began.

"You carefully avoided gender in describing the Weeper. I conclude—"

"The Weeper may be a man or a woman," said Karpo. "It might have been a man weeping in a high voice or a woman."

They were standing in the hall now near a window open to let in some touch of air in the summer heat. The moist taste of coming rain prickled Rostnikov's cheek and gave him a curious satisfaction. The sound of barking German shepherd dogs in the police kennels below the window gave a faraway sense of melancholy to the scene.

"Emil," Rostnikov said, walking at the side of the taller, gaunt man whose limp left arm was plunged into the black sling under his jacket, "have you ever read *The Adventures of Huckleberry Finn*?"

"No," said Karpo as they stepped aside to let a uniformed young man carrying a stack of files hurry past them. "Should I?"

"There is a passage in which the drifting young boy hears the faraway sound of someone chopping wood," Rostnikov said. "The sound of something far away, the echo of each plunge of the ax blade into the wood. It is a passage of great beauty, Emil. It is a passage which vibrates like a summer day in Moscow."

"I see," Karpo said, unable to fathom the cryptic turns of mind of the limping, near block of a man at his side. Porfiry Petrovich Rostnikov was an enigma in the life of Emil Karpo but one that the younger man accepted, for he respected his superior's abilities.

But Karpo knew that Rostnikov was not infallible. Occasionally, he failed to see something, to detect. The example was immediate. Rostnikov obviously had no idea that Karpo planned to make himself the next target of the rooftop Weeper.

Sasha Tkach had a headache. He was not much given to drinking vodka. He was well aware of the damage it did to those around him, and he often had the impression that at night Moscow was a vast matrix of drunks who staggered about like giddy or morose zombies. He had heard that it was worse in other countries—Iceland, the United States—but Moscow surely had a high percentage of those who sought escape in alcohol. One of those who did so was his neighbor Bazhen Surikov, the carpenter. Surikov liked to suggest that he was a painter. He wore a small beard like a caricature of a 1920s Parisian artist and even dabbled in painting, though Sasha thought the few works he had seen by the wiry man were at best mediocre. However, Sasha did not consider himself an art expert. He did, however, consider himself a man with many problems.

He and Maya had not exactly quarreled the night before. She had attempted to talk about their future, and he had attempted to avoid it. He was tired, sore from the bout with the blacksmith, angry at his assignment, and unable to think of a solution to the problem of what to do when the very visible child in Maya's stomach decided to face the world.

Sasha's mother, Lydia, offered no help, only her usual wisdom. "It will work out. Each day passes, and a new one comes. We have bread on the table, shoes on our feet, a bed to sleep on."

One could not quarrel with such wisdom, especially when one's mother was nearly deaf and interested in preserving platitudes rather than coping with reality.

And so when Bazhen Surikov had suggested that Sasha join him in his apartment to look at a new painting, Sasha had gone, leaving mother, wife, and soon-to-come child in their two-room apartment. And when Bazhen had shown him the idiotic painting of a horse or a boar or a bear on its knees, Sasha had been properly complimentary, which resulted in the offer by Bazhen of a shared bottle of vodka. Nearly two hours later, when Sasha had managed to return to his apartment, Maya looked at his smiling face and put down her book, undecided about whether to get angry or weep. She did neither but turned to go in the bedroom, realized her mother-in-law was in there, and then faced Sasha with a pleading look that said clearly, "See, I have no place to go when I am hurt, angry. And soon there will be a baby, your baby."

The next day, the vodka was no longer in effect, the sun was hot, and Sasha had no heart to pretend that he was the spoiled son of a member of the Politburo. He had some sense, he thought, of how an actor must feel who has a hangover, an ulcer, a nagging wife, and a dying friend and who must still step upon the stage to pretend for two hours that he is Alexander the Great.

Sasha had already had a meeting with Porfiry Petrovich Rostnikov; he had gone to two locations on his list and crossed out both, convinced that they were not what he was searching for. He had been especially disturbed by the fact that in his early-morning meeting, Porfiry Petrovich, who usually gave suggestions and attention and consideration to even minor cases, seemed to be indifferent to Sasha's investigation in spite of the fact that pressure was now being exerted because "an important official" had been the victim of the car thieves.

Sasha had taken the green metro line, the Gorkovsko-Zamoskvoretskaya line, to the end, gotten off at Rechnoi Vokzal, and wandered in unfamiliar territory in search of the building from which it had been reported that a large new car had been seen. The report was almost two weeks old and had come from a woman who, the report noted, was a notorious local busybody, the kind who would come up to you on the street and tell you to straighten your tie. Sasha Tkach knew the type; one of them had married his father and now lived in Sasha's small apartment.

Finding the building was difficult, but he continued. The directions had been poor, but find it he did, a one-story brick building that looked as if it had once been a small factory. There was a large car or truck entrance with a sliding metal door closed over it. The windows of the building were dirty, and one could not see because the curtains were closed. It meant nothing, this twenty-third location he had checked in two weeks while others were seeking snipers who shot policemen and mysterious old gunmen who stole candlesticks. Life was not always fair.

Sasha found a door at the side of the building, blinked once, sighed deeply, feeling sorry for himself, knocked, and entered before someone could say, "Come in," or, "Stay out."

Beyond the door, Tkach found himself facing a quite beautiful blond young woman, full and athletic looking, who wore no makeup and needed none.

"That door is supposed to be locked," she said, her eyes meeting Sasha's. "This is a private club for potential automobile mechanics."

Tkach looked past her without letting his eyes roam. There was a wooden partition behind them, a dirty wooden partition painted gray, behind which he could hear the scraping of machinery, the clanking of metal on metal. There was something defiant and attractive about the young woman holding a small wrench in one hand, her other hand on her hip. Even the smudges of dirt on her dark overalls were somehow appealing. A shiver of fear and physical attraction passed through the detective, and he felt confident that if he had not finally found what he was looking for, he had surely stumbled upon something the woman was trying to hide.

"My name is Pashkov," he said as the woman grabbed

his sleeve to turn him toward the door. "Your address was given to me by a mutual acquaintance who made me promise not to reveal his name."

"I don't know what you are raving about," she said, her face close to his, close enough to him to smell her and close enough for her to sense his slight trembling, the trembling of a wicked hangover.

"My father is a member of the Politburo," Sasha said quickly and thickly as she opened the door and pointed out with her wrench.

"How fortunate for you," she said sarcastically.

"I'm looking for an automobile," he tried, standing in front of the door. "A very good automobile."

She didn't slam the door. He tried to fix a slightly vapid smile on his face as he examined her. Her fine smooth face almost hid her emotions, but Tkach had been an investigator for almost six years, and he saw suspicion flicker in her eyes. He saw no sign, however, of fear and decided that in many ways this was a most formidable and admirable woman.

"Who sent you here?"

"No," he said, shaking his head. "No names. I don't want yours. You don't want mine."

"I already have yours."

"I forgot," Tkach said. "I was drinking with a friend last night—"

"Come back in," she said, reaching out to lead him back through the door. Before she closed it, she stepped out and looked around. Tkach watched her with admiration. A woman like this could take charge, find apartments, cars, get things done, and have time left over for massive warmth and babies.

"I'm looking for a car for myself," he said when she faced him. He spoke above the noise beyond the gray partition. "I'm willing to pay reasonably, and if things work out, I have friends who might also be willing . . ."

She was examining his face intently. Sasha was well aware of it, but he did his best not to reveal what he was seeing.

"If you are the police," she said slowly, "then you can simply have this building examined when you leave here. In that case, there would be no point in denying what we have here."

"Wait," Sasha said, stepping forward, uncomfortably warm, wanting to loosen his absurd tie.

"If you are who you say you are, however," she went on, paying no attention, "then we might as well attempt to negotiate. You are good-looking enough, but you don't strike me as either discreet or terribly intelligent."

Tkach's vodka tremor turned to anger, but he controlled it, recognizing that the woman might be testing him. In one sense, it didn't matter. She had as much as confessed, and she was quite right: all he had to do was force his way past her, go to the nearest phone, and have the place surrounded in a few minutes. But now he wanted to play this game through, to beat her. If it was chess they were to play, he wanted her respect when the game was over.

"I'm not accustomed to insults," he said, letting some of his anger out. "I went to Moscow University. I am certified in economics. I—" he fumed angrily, hoping that he was playing his role with indignation.

A smile touched the quite lovely full lips of the woman. Tkach did not like the smile or the words she spoke.

"Come," she said. "I'll show you some cars, and perhaps we can make a deal."

At this point Tkach considered that it might be wiser to concede the chess game and win the war, but he did not get beyond the consideration. He felt the presence behind him and knew it was confirmed by the woman's blue eyes that glanced over his shoulder. Someone was behind him, someone who would surely stop him or attempt to stop him if Sasha went for the door.

"Good," Tkach said, sighing. "Do you have a drink of something? I've come a long way."

He turned toward the wooden partition from beyond which the noise continued to come and found himself almost nose-to-nose with a man with a flattened, slightly red nose, a burly, rugged-looking man, and straight black hair falling over his forehead. He was well muscled, surly looking, and not at all pleased by the look that the woman was now giving to Sasha Tkach, whom she was beginning, apparently, to accept as someone she might well enjoy playing a game with.

On Gorky Street, across from the Central Telegraph Office, is the Moscow Art Theatre. The building is decorated with reproductions of the Orders of Lenin and the Red Banner of Labor awarded to the company. There is also a banner with the image of a seagull, the emblem of the theater, adopted from Chekhov's play, which had its premiere at the Moscow Art Theatre. There are two other buildings of the Moscow Art Theatre, one on Moskvin Street, the other on Tverskoi Boulevard.

The Moscow Art Theatre was founded in 1898 by the theoretician-director Konstantin Stanislavski and Vladimir Nemirovich-Danchenko. Both Chekhov and Gorky were associated with the theater, which continues to specialize in the plays of the two authors.

Rostnikov had been in the theater only three times before this Saturday morning's visit. It wasn't that he disliked theater. On the contrary, he enjoyed the idea of theater, but his interest lay not in traditional performance but in those works that generated the energy of other places.

He had left word in Petrovka about where he was heading and had taken advantage of his temporary restoration to authority by ordering a car and driver and indicating that it was by order of the deputy procurator. The police garage had not questioned him, though the car had been five minutes late, during which time Porfiry Petrovich had stood in the street, making people uncomfortable by trying to imagine what crimes they were capable of. Murder, he knew, was within the scope of anyone, given the proper motive or circumstances. He never searched faces for murder. It was the pickpockets, robbers, and car thieves he tried to imagine behind the somber passing faces.

Tracking down Lev Ostrovsky had proved to be quite easy. The All-Russia Theatrical Society had furnished an address and the information that Ostrovsky, though he was eighty-three, still worked at the Moscow Art Theatre. So Rostnikov had sat back, watching the tall streetlamps hum past as the faceless driver went down Gorky Street and turned at the Art Theatre passage.

Getting inside proved slightly difficult. He had told the driver, a young man with a bulbous nose, to wait at the car. The man, in uniform, had nodded without expression. It had not only occurred to Rostnikov that the driver might be either a KGB man or an informant for the deputy procurator; it had been a certainty. Since Porfiry Petrovich's unofficial demotion, he was watched, reported on, considered by various offices, each working separately, building files, wasting the time of many people. But, Rostnikov mused as he limped away from the locked front door and searched for a stage entrance, what useful work might they otherwise be performing, these people who spied on him? Perhaps they could be loaded on a truck and sent to Yekteraslav to work in the vest factory.

Washtub, he thought to himself, finding a heavy wooden door that did open, *you fantasize too much. It will make you dream. Dreams will turn to hopes. Hopes will turn to longing. Longing will turn to despair. Despair will turn to laughter. And laughter will get you in trouble*.

Beyond the wooden door, Rostnikov entered a dark world. A vast, high, dark world in contrast to the burning summer brightness of the outside. The smell of theater struck him. It was like old wood and comfortable carpeting and paint. His eyes adjusted and turned to the voice addressing him.

"What is it you want?" The speaker was a young woman in a black dress, her hair pulled back and tied with a black ribbon. She was vulpine beautiful, a type of face that suggested weary cleverness, of having seen so much that a little more would not be surprising. Her words challenged him to come up with a tale.

He reached into his rear pocket and grunted out his identification, noticing that his leather wallet was bulging and frayed. The bulge came partly from the bills he carried for needed purchases and partly from his unwillingness to part with little bits of paper on which notes were written to remind him of various things he never got around to doing.

The young woman's eyes darted at the wallet and back to his face. He had no doubt that she had actually looked at the card. She appeared to be quite unimpressed. "I repeat, comrade inspector. What is it you want? We are in production at the moment and have—"

"Lev Ostrovsky," he put in, looking around now that he could see. He was standing in a narrow corridor with a string of lights heading deep inside the building. To each side of the corridor were doors, but he could make out no sounds within them.

"I don't—" She began with a sigh, which Rostnikov recognized as the prelude to dismissal.

"You will," he assured her, cutting in again. It was time to assume a new role. "Lev Ostrovsky is here. I wish to see him immediately. I do not have time to watch you perform. I am in a good mood, a remarkably good mood considering many things I have no desire to share with you, but that mood can so easily become—" He held up his thick right hand palm down and let it flutter like a wounded bird.

The young woman folded her arms across her small breasts and let out her third sigh of the brief conversation. Rostnikov decided that she was not an actress. Her repertoire of mannerisms was too limited. Either she was without experience or simply had not cultivated her talents.

"Down this corridor," she said through closed teeth and over a very false cordial smile. "Turn left at the end and then right."

With that she turned and walked to a door, her heels clicking on the wooden floor, and made her exit.

Rostnikov, uncertain of the directions she had given, limped down the corridor, listening for the sound of a voice, a movement. When he had turned the second corner and was headed toward a door to his right that said Stage Entrance, he heard the sound of music.

He went through the door to the stage, following the music, moved up a low flight of stairs, and found another door. Beyond this door was the rear of the stage. The music was louder, an orchestra. It was familiar and not familiar. The backstage area was even darker than the corridor. Rostnikov moved carefully toward a light ahead that accompanied the music. Beyond a chair and a bank of switches for lights, Rostnikov found himself to the right of the stage of the theater. On the stage, illuminated by an insufficient light from high above, stood a man with a mop. On a chair near the old man was an old record player. The volume was very high and the man very old.

"Lev Ostrovksy?" Rostnikov shouted over the music, but the bent man simply soaked his mophead from the pail in front of him and kept his back to the policeman. Rostnikov could see in the dim light the drying soapy trail on the polished wooden floor of the stage. Beyond the dim light in darkness were hundreds of seats. He listened to his voice break against the far wall of darkness.

The old man did not turn immediately as Rostnikov stepped forward and turned off the record player. Silence thundered, and Rostnikov was suddenly aware of the mop squeaking over the floor.

It took the old man a beat or two to realize that the music was gone. He straightened and turned to face Rostnikov. There was a slight smile fixed on the ancient face, a smile that Rostnikov recognized as not one of amusement of the moment but the permanent mask some people wore. He was a short man in trousers held up by suspenders over a long-sleeved blue work shirt. He grasped his mop in two hands and pursed his lips as he examined the heavy man in front of him.

"What was that music?" Rostnikov asked, but the old man simply continued to stare. So Rostnikov shouted his question again.

"The soundtrack from *Rocky,*" Ostrovsky said in a willowy voice as he looked at the record player.

"Rocky?" asked Rostnikov, feeling as if he were in some absurdist play and that hundreds of first-nighters were just behind the light, trying to suppress coughs of laughter.

"An American moving picture," Ostrovsky explained. "I bought it from an American. Actually, I traded for two tickets to *Vassa Zheleznova*. I got the better deal."

Rostnikov nodded in agreement, partly to preserve his voice and partly because he could think of no appropriate rejoinder.

"'He reminds me of a policeman'," the old man said, his smile still fixed, his right hand leaving the mop to point at Rostnikov. "'A policeman I once knew. In our theater in Kostroma we used to have a policeman—a tall fellow with bulging eyes. He didn't walk. He ran, didn't just smoke but practically choked on the fumes. One got the impression he wasn't so much just living as jumping and tumbling, trying to reach for something quick. Yet what he was after, he himself didn't know.'"

"I'm—" Rostnikov said, but he had forgotten to shout, and the old man continued, no longer looking at the policeman but out into the audience.

"'When a man has a clear objective, he proceeds toward it calmly. But this one hurried. And it was a peculiar kind of haste—it lashed him on from within—and he ran and ran, getting in everybody's way, including his own. He wasn't avaricious. He only wanted avidly to do all he had to do as quickly as he could. He wanted to get all his duties out of the way, not overlooking the duty of taking bribes. Nor did he accept bribes. No, he grabbed them in a hurry, forgetting even to thank you. One day he got himself run over by some horses and was killed.'"

The old man turned to face Rostnikov, who was now convinced that he was dealing with senility and had best be simply polite and depart.

"Did your policeman have a name," Rostnikov said. "This one does." He pulled out his wallet and displayed it, though the man had obviously recognized him for what he was.

"There was no policeman," Ostrovsky said, shaking his head. "I was acting. You couldn't tell I was acting? That's the goal, the very thing all these young actors miss the point of. That business about the policeman was one of

Tatyana's speeches from Gorky's *Enemies*. Have you ever seen it?"

"No," Rostnikov admitted. The stage was cool, and the chief inspector half expected the ghosts of past audiences to reveal themselves and laugh at his confusion.

"Too much talk," the old man said, holding up his arthritic right hand and opening and closing it to show what talk was. "But I got you, huh? I can still act circles around these people today, these actors."

He demonstrated his ability to act circles around those who frequented the stage by swirling his mop in a circle on the floor.

"I can see that," Rostnikov said.

"I actually met Anton Chekhov when I was a boy," Ostrovsky said, pointing to a spot on the stage where he presumably met Chekhov. "Right here."

"Chekhov died before you were born," Rostnikov said.

"Then it was Tolstoy I met," the old man said with a shrug.

"Abraham Savitskaya," Rostnikov said. His leg was beginning to stiffen. He shuffled to the single chair on the stage, moved the record player to the floor, sat, and looked up at the old man, who had been struck dumb by the name from antiquity.

"He's dead," said Ostrovsky, his permanent smile going dead.

"How did you know?" Now Rostnikov was directing, acting to the nonexistent audience. He was back in his familiar role.

"Everyone's dead." The old man shrugged. "I have a stage to mop."

"Mikhail Posniky," Rostnikov shouted as the old man made a move to resume his work. The name stopped his motion. Rostnikov had a few more he could pull out if need be.

"Dead," Ostrovsky said.

"No, I think he murdered Abraham Savitskaya two nights ago here in Moscow."

"I haven't seen either of them for . . . a thousand years," Ostrovsky said. "Who can remember—"

"You remember lines from old plays."

"Ah," the old man said, his smile strong and crinkly. "That is fantasy, easy to recall. Reality, now that is not nearly as real to an actor."

How long could an eighty-year-old man stand up? It was an experiment that Rostnikov might have to make to get some answers.

"A brass candlestick," Rostnikov said. "Do you remember a brass candlestick that Abraham Savitskaya owned?"

The old man's face looked blank, and he began to shake his head when an image came, a memory. He shuffled a foot for new balance.

"No, it was Mikhail who left with the candlestick," he said, seeing some vague image in the past. "Mikhail and Abraham left together, going to America, they said. Each had a little suitcase, and Mikhail had the candlestick. His mother had given it to him just before he left. Why do I remember such things, such details? Who wants to remember such things?"

Rostnikov had no answer, only questions. "And have you seen either of them since they left the village, left Yekteraslav?"

"Who?"

"The men, Posniky or Savitskaya."

Ostrovsky shrugged. "Rumors—I heard rumors from people I ran into from the village, just rumors, rumors, rumors. You know rumors?"

"I know rumors," Rostnikov admitted to the parched mask of a smiling face that moved slowly toward him. "What kind of rumors?"

"That Mikhail had become a big gangster in America, just like the movies. Tiny Caesar, the Goldfather. Guns. Everything. It was possible. Who knew? He was a hard boy, a hard young man. I was a clown."

"Savitskaya?"

"Ah," Ostrovsky said, moving close enough to whisper. "A *macher.*"

"A *macher*?"

"That's Yiddish," Ostrovsky confided. "A dead language for dead Jews like me. Savitskaya was a dealer, a man not to be trusted."

"One more name," Rostnikov said, standing up. "A fourth young friend of yours from the village. Shmuel Prensky. What became—"

Rostnikov had simply been finishing the routine, looking for another step, another lead. He had not anticipated the reaction. Lev Ostrovsky went an enamel white and trembled. The smile became a grimace of pain or fear.

"Dead," Ostrovsky said, holding his mop handle, his knuckles twisted and white.

"When did he—"

"Long ago. He is dead, quite dead. Buried. Long ago."

"Yuri Pashkov still lives in Yekteraslav," Rostnikov pursued, walking over to the old man, ready to grab him if he should fall. "Pashkov—you remember him. He also seemed afraid of the name of Shmuel Prensky."

"Afraid? Me?" Ostrovsky said with a false laugh. He was acting quite poorly now. His reviews, if he survived the terror he was going through, would not be approving. "Shmuel Prensky is dead. I'm a very old man in case you haven't noticed. I have nothing to be afraid of from anyone on this earth. I've played the great roles. On this very stage I played Grigory Stepanovich Smirnov in Chekhov's *The Boor*. And I'd still be acting if they let Jews have decent roles. See, I'm not afraid to tell a policeman such things. So how could you—"

Rostnikov closed his eyes and opened them with a little shrug. "Perhaps I was mistaken," he said.

"Mistaken," the old man said vehemently. He began to mop the floor without bothering to dip it into the water. Then a thought struck him, and he turned, trembling.

"Gorky himself," he said, sweeping the darkness with his hand, "said the Art Theatre is as marvelous as the Tretyakov Gallery, St. Basil's Cathedral, and all the finest sights of Moscow. It is impossible not to love it."

"I can see that," Rostnikov said, watching the man justify himself to himself.

"It's enough to simply be in here, to be on this stage, to play out a little scene between soaping. To live out my last days with no trouble."

"I understand," Rostnikov said.

"'Life,'" said the old man almost to himself, "'has gone by as if I had never lived. I'll lie down a while. There's no strength left in you, old fellow; nothing is left, nothing. You addle head.'"

"Firs's final speech in *The Cherry Orchard*," Rostnikov said. "A fine performance."

"Thank you," Ostrovsky said, some of his spirit and color returning. "But—"

The old man was looking over Rostnikov's shoulder behind the stage, and Rostnikov turned to watch his uniformed driver hurry toward him. The man or the uniform had brought the fear back into Ostrovsky's eyes.

"Comrade inspector," the young man with the flat face said, ignoring the setting and the ancient actor. "You have a message, an urgent message from Investigator Zelach."

"Coming," Rostnikov answered, and then to the old man, he said, "Perhaps we will discuss ancient history and the life of the theater at some point in the future."

"My pleasure," said Ostrovsky, his smile broadening, his manner making it clear that such an encounter would not be a pleasure at all.

Rostnikov followed the driver toward the wings. He couldn't keep up with the younger man, not with his bad leg. Instead, he relied on that which he always relied on, his steady movement. He would bear in mind Gorky's detective from Kostroma; he would endeavor to move with caution and not get himself killed by runaway horses.

Behind Rostnikov, Lev Ostrovsky waited, waited a full five minutes, waited cautiously in case it was some trick and the policeman was hiding in the darkness. He forced himself to finish the floor, to make straight lines of soapy water, to set up the record player again, to listen to the martial music from *Rocky*, to control himself, to act out the role of cleaning man, a role he wanted to continue for whatever days he might have left. He waited a full five minutes, and then, when he was confident that he was again alone, he put down his mop, turned off the record player, and hurried off to find a telephone.

"Old, it's an old rifle. What can I say?"

Karpo watched Paulinin searching through the drawer of his desk in the laboratory on the second level below ground of Petrovka. Paulinin was wearing a blue smock and looked more like a flower seller in Dzerzhinsky Park than the eclectic encyclopedia he was. Paulinin looked rather like a bespectacled, nearsighted monkey with an oversized head topped by wild gray-black hair. He was forever searching for something, putting things together, looking for challenges. His office was a clutter—piles of books, objects from past investigations. Here a pistol with the barrel missing. There, on the tottering pile of books on the edge of the desk, some false teeth.

"You can," said Karpo, standing in front of the desk, motionless, "tell me when it was made, who made it, how I might discover who it belongs to."

"Miracles," said the monkey of a man, pulling a long wire from the drawer, examining it carefully with a squint and returning it. "The man wants miracles."

And miracles, Karpo knew, were just what Paulinin liked to deliver. And so he waited patiently, immobile, a dark tower around which buzzed the clever spider monkey.

Paulinin pushed the drawer closed, tapped both open palms on the paper-covered desk, and considered. An idea struck, and he shoved a report on coarse yellow paper aside and grabbed a syringe as if it might try to scurry off the table.

"An 1891–30 Moisin, our primary rifle of the last war with the Germans," Paulinin said, holding the syringe up to examine it against the ceiling light. "There are thousands still around. Amazing that this one can still shoot. The bullet went through an almost smooth barrel. The whole rifle is a relic. I don't see how anyone could hit the Kremlin—forgive my example—with it, let alone a policeman fourteen stories below."

Paulinin turned his back to place the examined syringe on the small sink in the corner.

"Go on."

Karpo's arm had in the past several days begun to lose all feeling. It had to be placed by him in the black sling like a sleeping baby each morning. He wondered if the numbness would continue to spread up his shoulder to the rest of his body. There was no fear in his conjecture, only a curiosity and a suppressed regret deep within.

"So," Paulinin said, turning to face Karpo and folding his arms as he leaned back against the sink, "the gun does not break down. It does not come apart, to be placed in a little carrying case. This is no—what was that American movie?"

Karpo did not go to movies, had only seen part of one while pursuing a pickpocket in the Rossia Theatre five years earlier.

"*Filthy Harry*," Paulinin said. "That was it. Americans are rifle crazy since Kennedy. Movies, books, full of rifles, full of people shooting people from rooftops. Like your Weeper."

"The rifle could not be broken down for transport," Emil Karpo reminded Paulinin, who pushed away from the sink and began to search through the pile of books on the desk.

"Your Weeper has to carry the rifle around full length. It is 51.5 inches long and weighs 8.8 pounds without a bayonet. It's not some little thing, either. Big, long, a Cossack penis, we used to call them. So, ask yourself, Comrade Karpo, how did your Weeper carry that rifle up to those roofs and down? What did your killer carry it in? A rolled-up rug, what? It's too big for a violin case like they used in old American movies."

"I've made a note," Karpo said, and found Paulinin pausing to catch his eye. Normally, Karpo took detailed notes and went back to his room to transcribe them, but with one hand it was a difficult task, and he wanted no comment or glance from Paulinin. They were not friends. In truth, Karpo, the Vampire, the Tatar, wanted no friends. He wanted no obligation except to the state.

Paulinin looked at the limp arm through his thick glasses and shrugged before continuing.

"So your killer is left-handed. The Moisin has a right twist, but his bullet enters, drifts toward the left. Could be done by a right-handed shooter, but someone who is picking a target will usually wait till the target is neutral or to the right. This is conjecture, of course, based on experience."

"Of course," agreed Karpo.

"Finally," said Paulinin, holding up a finger as he found the thin report he was searching for. "Your killer is strong. That rifle kicks like a member of the Supreme Soviet denied an extra box of American cigarettes. So, a picture is forming, comrade inspector?"

"Someone strong, probably big, left-handed, carrying something long enough to hide a long, heavy rifle."

"That's it," agreed Paulinin, adjusting his glasses and reexamining the report in his hand. Karpo was clearly dismissed.

"Very good," the detective said, not in the least offended by his dismissal. "If—when I find the rifle, I will bring it to you for positive identification."

Paulinin laughed and shook his head. "You are looking for an antique, Comrade Karpo, a mastodon. If you find it, there will be little need to verify its relation to the crimes. If you dragged the corpse of Stalin in here and said, 'Is this the Stalin who sat on your mother's face, the Stalin who wore his collar too tight, the Stalin who was the premier of all the Russians?' what could I answer?"

"You could answer like any Russian, 'It is possible,'" Karpo said, opening the door to depart.

Paulinin was actually surprised. Never in his fifteen years of dealing with the pale, sharp bone had he known Karpo to display any humor. He turned to his report on chemical testing of vomit with professional joy as soon as the door was firmly closed.

But Karpo had meant no humor in his remark. Humor was far from his mind. It was caution he voiced, a caution he usually exhibited but which something within him now told him, urged him, to abandon. Time was, he feared, against him. The Weeper might strike again, kill another policeman. Or Karpo's arm might be exposed, and he might be summarily dismissed. That could not, must not, happen till the Weeper was found.

He spoke to no one as he climbed the stairs. Karpo never took an elevator unless ordered to or accompanying a superior. He liked his feet on something solid. He walked home in the noon heat, absorbing but not considering the sweating figures that moved past him in shirt-sleeves or short-sleeved, loose blouses. The young woman who stared at him at the corner registered deeply but not consciously. Her breasts were large, unfettered, distracting. As he crossed Sverdlov Square and strode through the thin crowd in front of the metro station, the image of Mathilde came to him. He stopped, drew a deep breath, and willed the image to depart. He imagined a silver circle, breathed easily, ignoring the man with the loaf of bread under his arm who stared at him, and waited while the distraction of the body passed. When he moved again, he knew it would have to be addressed, that imp inside. There was no denying the animal inside. It could distract but it also confirmed, reminded. It spoke and had to be answered, or it would play hell with even the most disciplined body, calling it from its duty. Better to respond, appease, recognize, than to suffer the distraction.

He got on the Marx Prospekt train and stood for the four stops till the Komsomolskaya Station. There were a few seats, but Karpo did not want to sit. He wanted the distraction of discomfort, relished the physical irritation to be overcome.

He departed from the train, walked slowly through the crowd, avoided bumping into a man in a railway uniform who carried a net bag filled with green apples, and headed for the long escalator. The station reminded him of an ancient time with its decadent upturned glass chandeliers, its arched columns, and curved white roof with decorative designs. He preferred the more efficient outer stations to these compromises with the past.

Ten minutes later he stood in front of his room at the rear of the fifth floor of an apartment building built less than thirty years ago and already smelling of mold and mildew. As he always did before he entered, Emil Karpo checked the thin hair at the corner just above the door hinge to be sure no one had entered the room. Only then did he insert his key and step into darkness.

The shade was, as always, drawn. There was nothing to see through the window beyond, nothing he wished to look at. He clicked on the light in the ceiling and moved to his desk to turn on the desk lamp. The room was remarkably small, small even for a poor Muscovite. It was almost a cell, a cell with a simple table desk, a bed that was little more than a cot, a hot plate in the corner, and shelves of notebooks, each with the same black cover, notebooks filled with legible handwritten reports on every investigation he had ever engaged in.

It was in such a room that Lenin had worked, and Emil Karpo did not find it constricting. On the contrary, he enjoyed the compactness, the wall that kept his energy imploded.

He sat, reached for the current notebook, opened it to the proper page with some awkwardness, since he had but one hand to use, propped the book open with another book, and began to write and to think as he wrote of the next move in his campaign to catch the Weeper.

SIX

SASHA SAT UP ON THE MATTRESS AND GROPED FOR something to cover himself, a blanket, something, but there was nothing within easy reach. He brushed his hair from his eyes and realized that he was covered with sweat. The room was small, about the size of a large office at Petrovka. It contained a worn mattress in one corner, on which Sasha was now sitting; metal shelving, rusted and cluttered with bits of wiring, machinery, and dusty cans; a very battered table covered with automobile parts; and the woman named Marina, who stood calmly and quite as naked as Sasha, at least from the waist up. She was about to pull her blouse over her head, and Sasha observed with quite conscious guilt that her breasts were much fuller, much larger and rosier, than those of his own Maya.

He watched her pop her head through the blouse and shake her hair clear. She didn't look at the naked policeman sitting on the mattress who had, for the moment, forgotten his elusive trousers.

The ceiling of the room was high. In fact, it stretched far above them, perhaps two floors, and since the partition that defined it as a room was made only of thin planks of wood, the sound of grinding machines in the room beyond easily penetrated the sanctum of this unlikely sexual space.

Marina didn't brush or comb her hair. With confidence she simply tossed her head like an unconscious animal that must clear its field of vision to watch for predators.

Sasha Tkach remembered his pants again, looked about,

saw them across the room on a chair near the cluttered table, and tried to urge his body to rise. He touched the hairs on his stomach with a solitary finger and brought it away damp.

Why he had come to this moment of confusion and embarrassment was not completely clear to Sasha Tkach. How he had come to it was as sharp and visual as a poster for increased production glued to the temporary wall outside the Bolshoi.

The woman, Marina, had questioned him, questioned him in painful detail, about his alleged father, the kind of automobile he wanted, the deal they could make. As she had led him through the small workshop with the sullen, muscle-bound man named Ilya at their side, Sasha had the distinct impression that Marina was playing with him, smiling to herself as if she had a secret. She stayed close to Sasha, sometimes touching him, once let her breast run against his arm as she pointed to two men who were spray painting a small Volga. The Volga was basically blue, but under the hand of the two goggled men in overalls, it was turning a deep blood red.

The work space, the factory, was not enormous, but it was large enough to hold five automobiles in various states of alteration. The most striking of the vehicles was a white Chaika suspended about eight feet in the air by heavy chains attached to the front and rear bumpers.

"So, Comrade—" she had said.

Sasha had completed: "Pashkov."

"Yes, Comrade Pashkov," she went on, leading him past two goggled men who glanced at him with Martian eyes. "So, what do you think? Anything here you or your wealthy friends would like?"

She had paused, hands on hips, to say this, and Sasha, playing his role, had glanced at her, thinking that there was some provocation in her tone, words, attitude, but deciding that it was simply the woman's normal tone or his imagination.

All he had to do at that point was to make some deal, any deal, not to appear too anxious, to remember to pause, even idle, and then get to a phone, for surely he had found what he had been searching for. All he had to do was play his role out for a few more minutes. He had looked over at the man called Ilya, who was uncomfortably close, his arms folded across his muscular chest, his eyes filled with suspicion.

"The Chaika," Sasha said. "It's just what I need. Perhaps we can make a deal for that and"—he shrugged, beginning to perspire in the closeness of the loud shop and the man and woman who wedged him in—"who knows, some additional vehicles for my friends."

"Fifteen thousand rubles," the man called Ilya finally said in a growl.

Sasha had looked around at the Chaika with interest and was about to agree when the woman, who had stepped very close to him, whispered with a smile, showing very white, large teeth, "Thirty thousand rubles."

"Thirty thou—," he began.

"Worth every ruble," she went on with that same smile. He could smell her breath on his face.

"I'll—" Sasha had said as Ilya picked up a very nasty looking electric tool of uncertain function, umbilically tied to the wall with a thick cord. There was anger in Ilya's face as he pushed a button on the machine and it roared into artificial life in his hands, a metal blade whirring noisily as the machine vibrated. Something in Ilya's look made it quite clear that he was experiencing at least antagonism and more likely hatred toward the potential customer. The source of that hatred might be resentment at Sasha's feigned wealth, suspicion that something was not quite correct, or jealousy of Marina's attention to him. Whatever it was, Sasha did not like the look of the whirring blade or the noise or the man or the fact that he was now effectively blocked from a clear run to the door through which they had come. He might be able to push past the woman. After all, Ilya was carrying a heavy tool in his hands, and the other two burly men seemed to be reasonably well occupied with their painting. But there were two doors to get through, either of which might have been locked behind him, and there were automobile body parts to leap over and perhaps here and there a small pool of oil on which he might slip. No, though the situation was uncomfortable, his best chance was to see it through, play the role, though he wished now that he had been better prepared for it.

"Comrade Pashkov," she had said at that point, taking his arm quite firmly, "let's go into the office and conclude our deal."

The man named Ilya had flipped a switch on the machine. It shook in his hands, sending it into a louder, angrier paroxysm that seemed to amuse Marina as she led Sasha through a wooden door and into the smaller cluttered room where he immediately saw the mattress in the corner. She closed the door behind them, her back to him a moment, possibly locking the door before she turned to face him, still that look of amusement in her eyes. It was at that point Sasha became well aware of the single drop of sweat on her upper lip, her quite full upper lip. The room was hot, and he felt dizzy. Had he his gun, he would simply have pulled it out and ended the whole charade, but he had purposely left it behind in case he might be searched or the bulge seen by an experienced criminal eye. Besides, he had expected no real danger. Even at this point he told himself that it was imagination, an imagination that any policeman felt in such a situation, the fear that his frail disguise had been penetrated, a sense of guilt at being the deceiver, though he was on the side of law and they were the criminals.

"We must arrange for a place of delivery," he said in as businesslike a manner as he could muster. "A street corner will be fine. I'll have the cash in a small box. You can count it, and I'll—"

It was at that point that she had begun to unbutton her tight jeans. Each metal button, shiny and silver, popped open.

"What—?" he began, but he knew just what she planned.

There was no way he could refuse without a mad story, and his failure to answer her earlier questions about his assumed family and life had already created a possible suspicion that he did not want to build upon by saying that he was impotent, ill, homosexual, or any of several possibilities that sprang to mind. As her jeans dropped to the stone floor, Sasha knew that in his heart of hearts he did not want an excuse. Not only did he have to play out this scene; he wanted to do so. His head was warm and aching. Nausea swirled within, and moments later they were on the mattress in the corner, his clothes discarded, the warm, firm body of the woman on top of him, the smell of her sweat in his face. There was no doubt from the beginning that the woman named Marina was in charge. She grunted, sweated, controlled, urged, kissed, almost smothered him in frenzy, and left him exhausted as she rose and strode across the room to retrieve her clothes.

And so now he sat naked, guilty, confused, and watched her button her American jeans.

"The delivery," he said, looking for his clothes and trying to gain some control of the situation. The thought struck him that when they were all arrested and brought to trial, the woman would certainly tell what had happened in the room. He didn't know if he could keep Maya from finding out. He could simply deny it had happened. The court might tell her to be quiet. Perhaps no trial would be necessary. He wished he had a towel to relieve his drenched body and clean away some of the feeling, but all that existed was a grimy sheet crumpled at the foot of the mattress.

"You have delivered," she said, looking down at him, mocking.

"The money, the automobile," Sasha said, now feeling at a distinct disadvantage with her dressed.

Marina smoothed her hair and shook her head slowly to indicate a negative.

"But—" Sasha began.

"There is no money, policeman," she said, her hands back on her hips. "At least I hope you are a policeman, and not KGB. I don't think you're KGB. You don't have the look, the confidence, and a KGB man would have had his background story better rehearsed, at least most KGB men. Even within the KGB there is, sadly, some incompetence."

Sasha got up and tried indignation.

"Look," he began, and she indeed looked, which made him stop and feel his exposure from the soles of his feet through his soul.

"I've always wanted to make sex with a policeman," she said, walking to the door. He considered leaping forward, stopping her if he could, and searching for a way, though he was sure there was no way out of this room but through the door through which they had come. The only windows were small and very high on the stone walls.

"You were not bad," she said, "though you could have participated more. You are remarkably passive for a policeman. Have you ever killed anyone?"

"Yes," he said, feeling the last possibility of his charade slipping away.

"Good," she said, beaming. "I like that. Until today, I have never been responsible for anyone's death. What is your real name?"

Sasha did not answer the question but inched toward the chair behind the table where he hoped he had thrown his clothes.

"There are policemen at the exits to this building," he said. "It is best if you simply gather a few things and urge your partners to come out with me."

She shook her head as if a small child had tried to play a trick on her.

"No," she said. "There are no policemen at the exits. You would not have gone through all this, would not be sweating quite so hard, if you were not alone. Shall I guess, my little policeman? You simply stumbled on us here. You and maybe others are making the rounds, checking places on your own."

"Make no mistake," he said, knowing that dignity was impossible without clothing.

"I'll make no mistake, policeman," she said. "Ilya will kill you, and we will cut you into little pieces, very little pieces, and bury the pieces deep below the floor."

With that, and before he could move or speak, Marina threw open the door. Beyond it stood a burly, sad-faced man in a rumpled suit who looked something like a massive washtub.

Porfiry Petrovich Rostnikov looked beyond the startled woman at the naked detective and pursed his lips. His head shook slightly, and Sasha realized that he could hear the man sigh. The sounds of machinery in the outer room had stopped. Sasha didn't know when it had happened.

"Put your pants on, Sasha," Rostnikov said.

"Inspector, I—" Sasha began, but Rostnikov interrupted.

"Pants, Sasha. Dignity."

Sasha went for the chair, found his pants, and began dressing quickly, without looking at what he was doing, pushing his sockless feet into his untied shoes, buttoning his shirt incorrectly.

Beyond Rostnikov, Sasha could see the man called Ilya and the other two in overalls. Their goggles were off their eyes and on their heads, pushing back their dark hair. All three were taller, younger, than the inspector, who seemed not in the least perturbed.

"He came to the door," Ilya explained to Marina. "Said he wanted to see the man who had come to buy a car. I didn't know—"

"It's all right," Marina interrupted, looking directly at the rumpled inspector before her with interest. "Inspector—"

"Rostnikov. Porfiry Petrovich Rostnikov," the inspector supplied. "Sasha, come."

Tkach stuffed his socks into his pocket, brushed his damp hair back, and hurried across the room, past Marina, and to Rostnikov's side. Ilya and the two goggled men stepped back a bit, confused, into the crowded shop but blocked the path to the door.

Marina, apparently unconcerned and quite curious, closed the door behind her.

"Inspector," she said, "I had planned to kill one policeman today, but you afford me the opportunity to kill two."

"Marina," one of the men in overalls said.

"We kill them quickly," she explained, "and go out the back through the apartment. It is what we planned from the beginning. These are the only two who have seen us. Even if there are more outside, once we are gone, no one knows our faces. We start again, Ilya."

Sasha looked at the sullen Ilya, who examined the younger policeman with quite obvious jealousy and hatred. Something metal and tarnished and heavy rested in Ilya's oilstained hand.

Marina's eyes met those of Rostnikov. She smiled, and he smiled back. There was something sympathetic in the man's eyes that she didn't like, that made her confidence falter. The man was about to die because she willed it, and yet he looked at her with—

"Do it," she said. "Do it and let's get out of here. Just leave the bodies on the floor and let's go before the others outside start breaking down the door."

Sasha stepped back and felt his bare ankle scrape against metal as Ilya raised the wrench to Rostnikov's back.

"No," Sasha screamed, and the Washtub stepped back quickly to the right. The wrench sliced across his shoulder, and the two men in overalls leaped forward to grab the inspector's arms. Sasha moved quickly forward toward Ilya and felt Marina's push. He felt himself tumbling over a blanket-covered engine. His back struck something hard and jagged, and he rolled over, trying to grab something, to help the inspector and himself. Panting, he looked up as Ilya stepped forward toward Rostnikov, whose arms were held by the two men, and made it quite clear that he planned to aim his large wrench more carefully.

The grunt Rostnikov gave was less of exertion than of minor concentration. His two arms came forward, taking with them the full weight of the men holding him. They barely had time for surprise to register. Their bodies collided, and Ilya brought the wrench down solidly on the shoulder of one of the two, who screamed in pain and panic.

The injured man let go of the inspector and grabbed for his broken shoulder while the other man continued to hold his grip on the policeman, which proved to be a mistake of the highest order. Sasha scrambled up and saw a calm look of satisfaction on the inspector's face as he grabbed the man in overalls with his now-free hand and lifted him off the ground to ward off Ilya's resumed attack. The injured man, meanwhile, staggered blindly toward the office door and crumpled, gripping his shoulder as Rostnikov, now carrying the bewildered man above him, advanced on Ilya. There was no strain on Rostnikov's face, though the man he held above him easily weighed two hundred pounds.

Sasha looked around for Marina and saw her duck behind the half-painted Volga. He staggered after her, skipping over the whimpering man with the broken shoulder and watching with fascination as the wrench-armed Ilya felt his way back from the advancing Rostnikov.

A pause, a beat, and with a slight grunt Rostnikov hurled the screaming man toward Ilya. The grimy missile struck Ilya, sending them both sprawling backward into and over a heavy automobile jack. Ilya scrambled, dazed, out from under the apparently unconscious man atop him and searched for a way of retreating from the patient, limping figure that moved toward him. Sasha would later swear that Rostnikov was humming, humming something that might have been Bach, though later Rostnikov would claim that it had been Vivaldi.

Marina was nowhere to be seen. Sasha moved around the Volga, looking behind machines and parts, into corners. He thought he saw a movement ahead but stopped when the sound of that whirring machine screamed behind him.

Across the room Sasha saw the steadily advancing Rostnikov less than a dozen feet from the now-wild-looking Ilya, who held the grinding saw in front of him. Ilya's muscles and T-shirt were dark with sweat.

"I'll cut you in half," he said through closed teeth, but Rostnikov, whose humming could no longer be heard, simply continued forward until the younger man had his back against the wall, the saw held out in front of him.

Something was said by Rostnikov that Sasha could not quite make out. He thought it was a patient "How long can you hold that?" or something equally conversational. He wasn't sure over the sound of the saw. If indeed that was the question, it was never answered. Ilya shouted and rushed forward, the saw in front of him. Rostnikov's left arm shot forward, his sleeve brushing the blade, which tore into the dark material. With his right hand, Rostnikov grasped Ilya firmly by the shirtfront while the inspector's left arm continued its movement and slapped the still-spinning saw away. The saw struck the floor, sending up sparks as it bit in frustration at the cement. The cord slithered, and it looked to Tkach like an angry snake with a whirring, screeching metal head slithering out of control.

Rostnikov held Ilya up in front of him with one hand as the younger man tried to free himself and punched at the thick arm. Rostnikov whispered something as the snakelike saw skittered and continued to scream until it hit the wall, let out a bright final flash of anger, and went quiet.

". . . were going to cut us into little pieces," Sasha could now hear Rostnikov saying. The man with the broken shoulder was sobbing very gently, feeling sorry for himself.

Ilya's T-shirt had begun to tear as he screamed, "Bastard," and swung again at Rostnikov. Rostnikov shook his head in disgust at the inability of men to learn from their mistakes. His arm came back, and with a slight grunt he sent the startled Ilya sailing through the air, his arms flaying behind him, trying to grab something, to look back at where he was going, but the flight was too short. He hit the wall with a sick thud and slipped down in an unconscious heap. There was a stain of blood on the wall where his head hit, and Sasha was sure that the man's head was at least broken, if he wasn't dead.

Rostnikov stood watching as Ilya shifted slightly, tried to rise, and failed, and sat back. Only then did he turn to look for Sasha, whose eyes met his across the room.

"The woman," Rostnikov said.

"I—" Sasha began, but never finished his answer.

"Here," she said, and the two men looked around, finding her at the same moment.

She stood next to an old wooden hoist dangling from the ceiling behind the Chaika in the air. The hoist was connected to the chains that held the Chaika in the air. Her hands on the hoist had set the dangling car slowly spinning like a massive white magnet seeking the elusive north. What troubled Sasha even more was that the slowly spinning car was directly above Inspector Porfiry Petrovich Rostnikov.

"You move and I drop the car," she said with a smile, her hands firmly on the lever of the hoist. "And I don't think you are fast enough with that dead leg to get out from under in time. What do you think?"

Rostnikov shrugged rather indifferently.

"We must deal," she said.

Her eyes were fixed on the inspector as Tkach slowly edged behind the Volga and moved behind her.

"What can we do?" Rostnikov said gently. "Would you believe my promises? You let go of that and we have you. You might crush me, it's true. I don't think I can make it out from under here in time, but what do you gain? You don't leave here free."

"But," she said, "I'll have the satisfaction of smashing one bear of a policeman and destroying someone important's beloved car."

Rostnikov glanced up at the car slowly spinning over his head and remembered Procurator Khabolov's look of concern about his beloved white Chaika.

"I don't like cars," Rostnikov said softly, conversationally. Moving slowly, carefully, Tkach knew that the inspector was stalling, giving him time and cover to move. Marina's grip on the hoist lever was firm, and for a horrible instant Tkach considered that his life might well be easier if he shouted, and let her crush Rostnikov, who had seen him naked and compromised. He could then simply murder Marina and—But it was only the next level of guilt upon guilt. He knew it was not in him to act on the evil thought. It came, went, was gone. He crept forward, very carefully.

"You are going to die, policeman," Marina said with a laugh. "Do you know that?"

"You mean I'm going to die eventually or now? The former I am well aware of and have come to terms with. Of the latter, who knows? The scene is not yet played."

Tkach was now about seven or eight feet away from her. He crouched next to the fender of the dark car. He could see the woman's fingers slipping on the lever and knew that whatever was to be done must be done quickly. If Rostnikov were to be crushed, would Sasha wonder if he had purposely made the wrong move?

"Policeman," she said with some admiration, "you are mad."

Rostnikov put up a hand—his left hand, with the sleeve that had been cut by Ilya's saw—and let it sweep the room.

"You are standing there with a dancing car threatening to kill me. Bodies are strewn over. You have no chance to get away, and you call me mad."

"Perhaps we are both mad," she countered.

"We are both Russians." Rostnikov sighed. "You will do what you will do."

The man with the crushed shoulder decided to let out a small whimper, and Ilya stirred slightly against the wall. The other man Rostnikov had thrown lay quite motionless.

Tkach tried to signal to Rostnikov as he stepped away from behind the dark car. He wasn't sure the inspector saw him, but he had no time to check.

"Marina," he shouted.

She turned quickly toward him, her hand touching the lever. The Chaika began to spin wildly as it jerked to a stop.

"No," she screamed, and Sasha stopped no more than four feet from her, hesitating, watching her hand on the lever, but she was too late. She turned quickly toward the space under the car and realized that Rostnikov had stepped back, limped just beyond the shadow of the massive weight dangling from the chains.

Her eyes met those of the inspector and asked a question. Tkach glanced at Rostnikov, who looked up at the car and shrugged.

Marina's hand pulled back as Tkach lunged for her, and the Chaika dropped on screeching chains, dropped with a massive crash, its front end hitting first and then its rear. Glass and metal exploded through the room, and Tkach threw himself to the floor. The Chaika and the car-theft operation were no more.

The pain was much worse that day than it had been the day before, but Vera had expected that. Actually, she welcomed it, for she had already committed herself, found meaning to the end of her life. If she were suddenly and miraculously to be cured, to discover it had all been a mistake, then the policeman and the others she had killed would have died for nothing. Well, not for nothing. The corruption would still have existed, but there would have been an irony she did not want to face. There was just so much irony a human can take, she thought as she finished putting the rifle in the trombone case, snapped the flimsy latch, and glanced over at her mother, who had fallen asleep over her sewing.

Adriana Shepovik snored gently, a slight breeze touching her face through the open window. Vera felt nothing for her. Then the pain in her stomach punished her and told her to feel. She tried, tried to imagine her mother alone, as she would be, but Vera could feel nothing but its truth. Vera would not be, and her mother would. Her mother would live without meaning, but she would live and suffer. She was good at suffering, had turned it into an old woman's art.

Vera took seven or eight deep breaths and then a series of short ones before taking five of her pills. She had bought the pills from a clerk in the medical-supply store. He had been furtive, demanded extra money, refused to give the name of the pills, insisting only that they would temporarily eliminate pain. He guaranteed it. He was right, but the pain stayed away for only short periods, and more and more pills were required to relieve it.

Vera made her way to the metro station and glanced at the sky as she went. There was the possibility of rain, which would be fine. Her original plan was to wander around till night and move to the station she had picked out, but the pain might come again. She didn't have much time. Maybe if it rained, if the rain came, it would grow dark, would provide an artificial night. She had a sense of incompleteness. It was like reading a newspaper. If a word from a story caught her eye, she had to read the whole story even if the subject didn't interest her or the story would haunt her. Things once begun had to be finished, and she had decided within herself that she must destroy at least one more soldier or policeman, one more at least. Was that too much to ask after what she had been forced to suffer? If a God existed, would he not grant her this wish, look down at her and say she deserved that satisfaction? If a God existed, he could simply take the soul of the policeman and do with it what he would do, anyway, at some point, as he would do with Vera's soul if one existed. Vera didn't think one existed. One's satisfactions and rewards and revenge came in this life, no other.

She tried to look at no one as she rode the subway, not even at the two sailors who talked in the far corner. She stood, swaying slightly with the movement of the car, trying to hold her upright trombone case close to her so no one would feel its weight and sense its shifting contents. At the Kropotkinskaya metro station, groups of young people carrying little bags jostled past her, hurrying toward the huge Moskva Swimming Pool. She let them flow by her and began her walk and her wait, wishing the sky to darken, hoping she could put off taking more of the pills, which, she knew, created a pleasant disorientation that might hamper her aim and shake her resolve.

She walked around the outside wall of the pool, listening to the screams and voices within. At the Kropotkin embankment beyond the pool she leaned over the stone wall and watched the boats going down the Moscow River. She watched for perhaps ten or fifteen minutes, grew restless, felt the pain returning, and started back toward Volkhonka Street. People sped past her now, but she moved across to the massive Pushkin Fine Arts Museum. She knew the story of the museum, had visited it frequently, particularly as a child in school when it was thought she had some artistic talent. The building had been erected at the turn of the century. It was, she knew, the largest museum in the Soviet Union outside of the Leningrad Hermitage.

She clutched the trombone case to her, ignoring the looks of guards and visitors. The crowd was large, and she let herself wander, seeing but not absorbing the Greek and Roman collection, the stone statues that would be there long after she was gone. Before she could begin to hate them, she wandered into the picture gallery where she stepped on the foot of a small boy, who screamed.

The boy's mother looked at Vera, ready to fight, but something in Vera's face stopped her, and she settled for, "That's all right, Denis. Some people are blind pigs."

Vera walked on past Botticellis, Rembrandts, Rubenses, Van Dycks, Constables, Gauguins, Picassos, and Van Goghs. Once they had given her satisfaction. Now they sickened her with their suggestion of timelessness. Vera would leave nothing behind her, no Olympic records, no paintings, her only art of creation one of destruction, a protest.

She had to take more pills. There was no help for it. She shifted the trombone case to her other hand and pulled the bottle out of her pocket. There were not many of the green pills left, perhaps a dozen or so. She would have to go back to the man who had sold them to her, the man who sickened her with his corruption. She placed the case between her legs, poured out some pills, threw them into her mouth, and forced them down dry. It was painful, but the pain in her dry throat distracted her from the pain in her stomach. She stood while people moved about her, the practiced move of Muscovites who watched without making it clear they were doing so. Everyone gave the impression of minding their own business except for a heavyset *babushka* who walked over and said, "If you're sick, you shouldn't be walking the streets. You should be home, not giving diseases to other people."

Vera looked at the angry old woman, who was saying exactly what her own mother would say to a stranger on the street. Either pretend the other person isn't there or walk right up to them on the street and chastise them for not sharing your moral commitment.

Vera looked at the woman with vague curiosity. She stared down the old woman, who eventually backed away, shrugging and angry.

The sky was darker when she stepped back outside, and she felt some sense of hope. It was going to rain. No doubt. It would rain. She felt dizzy, slightly dizzy, but also somewhat euphoric as she crossed Kropotkin Square and was almost struck by a bus at the corner of Gogol Boulevard. When she started down Kropotkin Street and passed the entrance to the Soviet Peace Committee Building, the sky rumbled distinctly.

"Let's hurry," a man growled at a young woman in high heels who gave him an angry glare as they passed Vera.

The street was filled with people, many people, especially soldiers. There were policemen, too, an ample supply. The trick would be to get to her destination, set up, and pick her target just before the rain came or just after it ended. During the rain people would get off the street. She would have to be clever, precise, careful. She would have to remember everything her father had told her about shooting.

She hurried, as well as her failing body would allow, toward her destination, ignoring the people she passed, thinking only of her task, trying to forget the painting in the museum. It had been by some minor English realist. She couldn't remember what the subject had been, a landscape surely, but what had been in it? It gnawed at her, told her to turn around, go back, complete it, but she didn't have the time. Not now. Not today. Perhaps later or tomorrow, if there was a tomorrow. There had to be a later or tomorrow. She could not end her life without knowing what was in that painting and without taking her father's rifle out one more time and finding the right target.

Even had she not been absorbed in her thoughts, even had she glanced back as the sky rumbled and darkened even further, it is doubtful that she would have noticed the tall, vaguely Oriental, pale man behind her with his right arm in a black sling.

Earlier that morning Emil Karpo had been sitting at his desk at Petrovka going over his file and waiting. He had prepared his description carefully and felt confident that it was more than guesswork. Rostnikov was nowhere to be found, and time was passing. He could have gone directly to the Gray Wolfhound, but he had no time or patience for clowns, and so he prepared his description and took it directly to each of the militia supervisors for each district, making it clear that they were to give it not only to those assigned to the various buildings but to all the police on the street, all the uniformed guards in public buildings, and all the officers who had taken up positions on key rooftops.

Emil Karpo was not a man to be ignored. Seven of his supervisors had simply accepted the description and agreed to pass it out quickly. They had no desire to prolong conversation with the Vampire, the Tatar with the dead brown eyes. It was easier to do what he requested. Besides, they might be the next victim of the Weeper, and it would be best to cooperate. A few of the military supervisors balked or sulked, but eventually they all agreed, and Karpo went back to his desk to drink cold tea and wait. The description had been simple. Look for a man or woman, of recognized size and strength, carrying a case long enough to hold a rifle. It might be a music case, a fishing case, anything. The person would probably be alone and might behave erratically.

By seven in the morning the reports had begun coming in. Karpo listened, believing it was too early in the day for the Weeper to appear but not taking any chances. He had actually dispatched two cars to pursue leads by noon, but they had proved negative. One had turned up a carpenter going to work, another a member of the ballet orchestra. At nine he discovered that the Gray Wolfhound had ordered the rooftop surveillance to begin at six that night, since the Weeper always struck at night. Karpo tried to reach Colonel Snitkonoy to get the surveillance to begin immediately, but the colonel was out. And then the call had come from the guard at the Pushkin Fine Arts Museum, and he was on his way after telling the guard to follow the woman and call her whereabouts back to the museum office where Karpo was heading.

The dispatcher of automobiles was surprised to get a call from Inspector Karpo. He couldn't remember a single time Karpo had ever ordered a car. The legend was that Karpo thought it a waste of Soviet dollars that could be better spent on real needs. The dispatcher, who felt uneasy even hearing the voice of the Vampire, responded without a word and assigned the driving task to one of the older officers whom he wanted to punish for a minor act of assumed insolence.

Karpo said nothing when the car pulled up in front of the building. He got in the back and cradled his senseless arm. His eyes caught those of the driver watching him in the rearview mirror, and Karpo stared back at the mirror, unblinking. He kept his dark eyes fixed on the mirror for five full minutes, so that each time the driver looked up, he saw his pale passenger solemnly glaring through him. The driver sped onward, wanting to get this assignment done as soon as possible and vowing never to get on the wrong side of the dispatcher again.

Luck had been with Karpo, though he did not think of it as luck. It simply happened. Had he not spotted the museum guard in the crowd on Kropotkin Street, he would have gone to the museum, waited for the guard's call, and eventually have caught up with the woman. But Karpo saw her, dark and heavy, carrying the case, walking like a somnambulist, her lips moving as she carried on a conversation with herself.

"Corner stop," Karpo said, and the driver gladly pulled

over with a screech, almost running down a couple with a small child between them. "Go back," Karpo said, and got out of the car. The car was gone before the pale policeman reached the sidewalk.

The uniformed guard was startled when Karpo tapped his shoulder. He let out a gasp, turned in fear, and recognized the assistant inspector. The guard was about fifty, his tie stained with sweat.

"She's—" he began.

"I see," Karpo said softly, watching the woman amble ahead, clearing a path with her trombone case. "Go back to the museum."

"I'll go back to the museum," the guard repeated, and Karpo moved past him through the crowd as the first drops of rain came from the dark, angry sky.

SEVEN

"AND SO I HAD OFFICER ZELACH FOLLOW ASSISTANT Inspector Tkach as a backup," Rostnikov explained as he sat in the chair in front of Deputy Procurator Khabolov's desk. "When Tkach took more than twenty minutes inside the building, Zelach followed instructions and called me. I—"

"My car," Khabolov said, standing suddenly behind the desk, his sad hound face quivering, his hands held behind his back to keep them from spasms of anger and frustration.

The office smelled slightly bitter, like the waiting room of a steam bath. When Anna Timofeyeva had occupied it, the office had always smelled to Rostnikov of tea and paper.

"Your car—" Rostnikov sighed sympathetically, shifting slightly to take some pressure from his leg. "Tkach and I risked our lives to save your Chaika, our very lives, but there was no dealing with the madwoman."

Khabolov's hand came out to accuse or attack, but he controlled it and raised the palm to push the stray hairs atop his head. The battle was joined and clear. Rostnikov would feign sympathy, and Khabolov would know he was lying but be unable to accuse him. Khabolov would pick, question, punish, but not allow his emotions to show, not let it be seen that he was punishing, though he knew that Rostnikov would understand. And so the two men faced each other and pretended.

"I appreciate your willingness to risk your very bodies

for material goods, Khabolov countered, returning his hand behind his back.

"I felt that the deputy procurator's official vehicle was more a symbol of the authority of the state than an item of personal and material satisfaction," said Rostnikov, somberly folding his hands on his lap.

Khabolov looked down at Rostnikov, searching for even a hint of insolence, but there was none there. The deputy procurator's eyes moved down to the report on his desk. He had to lean forward slightly to read it.

"You were unable to save my automobile, but you managed to break the shoulder of one suspect, the ribs of another, and the skull of a third."

"They resisted arrest."

"Do you expect the government to pay for repairs on your suit?"

Rostnikov looked down at his torn sleeve. He had been given no time to change clothes; instead, he had hurried back to Petrovka to write his report and get to the deputy procurator's office.

"Of course not," Rostnikov said. "It was, like your Chaika, ruined in the line of duty, but we must all make sacrifices for the state and accept our share of responsibility."

"You are an insolent man, chief inspector," Khabolov said, leaning forward with both hands on the desk.

"I am a weary man, comrade procurator, and I have a sniper and the killer of an old man to pursue. May I be excused?"

Khabolov's face flushed and turned red, though not quite as red as the flag that stood in the corner. His eyes went narrow, and Rostnikov recognized an official look designed to send fear into the guilty and nonguilty alike. Rostnikov was too weary to feign fear. He simply looked up placidly. The excitement of the morning had passed. The body fluids had coursed through Rostnikov in that makeshift garage. It had been no more than ten minutes, perhaps less, but it was such minutes that made being a policeman most enjoyable. Generally, so little was actually concluded, and that which was concluded normally came to pass through patience and paper and telephone calls and long hours of talking and compromise. Porfiry Petrovich felt tired and pleased. Even with his eyes open and fixed attentively on Khabolov, he imagined the falling Chaika and smiled deep within himself.

"You may not be excused," Khabolov said, sitting behind his desk to indicate a new phase of conversation. There was a heartbeat of hesitation in the dog-faced man that drew Rostnikov's interest.

"Chief inspector, you are to drop your investigation of the murdered Jew completely and concentrate on the Weeper."

"Very good," Rostnikov agreed. "I'll put it aside till the Weeper is caught and then—"

"You are to turn your files on the case over to me and drop the investigation completely and indefinitely—no, forever," Khabolov cut in with irritation.

"On my own time I would like to check the procurator's files for a—"

Khabolov was now perspiring, though the window was open, sending in a slight but adequate breeze. Something quite odd was going on, and Rostnikov began to observe his superior with curiosity.

"You no longer have access to the procurator's files," Khabolov said, reaching for a random file to indicate that the meeting had ended. With eyes down at the paper in his hand, he added, "For political reasons, which you may know."

There was no arguing with Khabolov. Rostnikov knew this. It wasn't that Khabolov couldn't be maneuvered, swayed, tricked. Given time, Rostnikov was sure he would solve the man, find ways to deal with him, but the abrupt air of the man, coupled with his clear nervousness, made it evident that the order to drop the investigation came from somewhere above Khabolov.

And so Rostnikov barely nodded.

"That is all," said Khabolov without looking up, and Rostnikov stood, propping himself up with the back of the chair, and moved slowly to the door and out. He had things to do, his jacket to change, and the murderer of Sergeant Petrov to catch. Perhaps the murder of Abraham Savitskaya and the mystery of the missing candlestick could wait. Perhaps.

By the time he got back to his tiny office, the rain had begun to fall. The single small window wouldn't open; it hadn't opened for months. Rostnikov had intended to fix it himself, though such initiative was frowned upon. There were repairmen assigned to such things, though the repairmen seldom came even after the proper forms were filed, approved, and forwarded. To get the window repaired through proper channels, Rostnikov would need the signature of Deputy Procurator Khabolov, and the price for such . . . Sitting behind his desk, Rostnikov smiled privately. A plan came. He watched the rain hit the window for about five minutes, doodled three-dimensional cubes of various sizes for a few more minutes, and scrawled out the work order to have the window fixed.

On the way out, he checked Karpo's desk, found a note indicating that Karpo was pursuing a lead, and called to Zelach, who sulked at his corner desk, his shaggy head hovering over a document.

"Zelach," Rostnikov said, moving past two investigators arguing over where they would have lunch. One of them, Irvinov, was a giggler. Everything seemed to amuse him—sex, food, death. His laughter was nervous and made Rostnikov uncomfortable. He had long ago decided that Irvinov's nervous laughter was much like that which Rostnikov's son, Josef, had displayed when he was a child. Josef had channeled the nervous laughter into a bemused, ironic smile. The thought of Josef softened him.

"Yes, Comrade Rostnikov," Zelach said.

"You did very well this morning," Rostnikov said gently. "You were instrumental in crushing that car-theft ring. I've just commended you to the deputy procurator. You have been noticed."

Zelach was not sure whether he wanted to be noticed, but the idea of being commended to the new deputy procurator was surely better than being reported for incompetence.

"Thank you, chief inspector," he said somberly.

Rostnikov stood with one hand on the small desk and handed Zelach the order for the window repair.

"Take this work order to the office of Colonel Snitkonoy. Tell them it needs the colonel's approval immediately, that it relates to the investigation, that I will soon be giving him a complete report."

Zelach took the work order and looked at it as if it were some radioactive treasure to be held in awe and handled with care.

"I'll do it immediately," Zelach said.

"Good man." Rostnikov sighed. "Good man."

And with that Rostnikov eased his way out of the large office and down the corridor. Emil Karpo was handling the Weeper. The automobile thieves were caught, and three other cases Rostnikov was working on were at a standstill. It would be, he decided, a good afternoon to make a few social calls, beginning with the strange daughter of the dead old man in the bathtub. Yes, it would simply be a social call, for he was officially off the investigation.

As he trudged through the rain, back straight, eyes unblinkingly fixed on the large woman carrying the trombone case, Emil Karpo felt an aching numbness that made him want to shift his arm as if he had slept on it for a generation or two.

Except for an occasional umbrella carrier or person so intent on getting somewhere that they braved the driving rain to dash from doorway to doorway, the lean detective and the woman were the only ones who seemed to be out in the rain.

Karpo welcomed the rain and the ache in his arm. Life was, after all, a test. The body was a papier-mâché vessel that had to be endured. Man proved himself, his worth, by accepting the weakness of the body and rising above it, not letting pain or emotion rule. Man, if he were to have dignity and meaning, had to rise above his animalism. An individual man was but a transient vessel. Mankind working together as a united organism had power and meaning.

The police were the white corpuscles of the body politic. If a cell went bad, an intruder threatened, the police officer, the soldier, stepped in and removed the offender. If the police officer were destroyed in the process, he would have achieved his goal, served his function.

Emil Karpo was not deluded. Crime would not stop. Corruption would not end. It was the nature of the human beast. It was inevitable. The goal of the Soviet state was a perfection it could never reach, but the seeking of that state of perfection created meaning. Each pain, setback, and criminal, bureaucratic obstacle simply proved the need for commitment.

They walked. First she seemed to have a destination in mind, but as the rain came down harder and harder, the large woman began to wander, her thin dress drenched and clinging to her sexlessly. She walked, and he followed, knowing he would follow for hours, even days, if he had to. He would follow, wait to be sure, and then end it. If by chance she proved to be innocent, he would prove that, too, go home, change clothes, and return to his office for more calls, more leads. He would wait and wait until he found the Weeper or was ordered to stop looking.

It was almost three in the afternoon when the woman began to move resolutely toward some destination. Her pace quickened, her head came up a bit, and she shifted her instrument case to her left hand. The rain had let up just a bit, and they were heading down Kutuzovsky Prospekt. She had not only moved within the possible pattern of previous attacks but was moving in the direction of the Ukraine Hotel.

Karpo was no more than twenty paces behind the woman when she stopped abruptly in front of Don Igrushki, the House of Toys, at 9 Kutuzovsky Prospekt. She turned and looked directly at the detective. The long strands of dark hair clung to her face. There was a madness in her eyes, a defiance that convinced Emil Karpo that he had not wasted his day. He continued to walk, not looking at the woman. She stood, feet firmly planted, not moving the wet, clinging hair from her eyes, nose, and mouth. She watched as he moved past, looking directly in front of her, and he continued down the street as if he had an appointment for which he could not be late. He knew her eyes were on him, knew she would watch him, wondering, cautious, but Karpo did not look back. He knew where she was going and planned to be there when she arrived.

Inside the lobby of the hotel, Karpo paused for a moment, scanning the faces that glanced up at him. The lobby was filled with people talking, waiting, wondering when the rain would end so they could get about their business or pleasure.

There were more than two thousand rooms in the twenty-nine floors of the hotel, with excellent views of Central Moscow from many of the windows. The view from the roof was especially magnificent, but tourists had no access to the roof. Karpo, tingling hand plunged deeply into his black sling, strode across the floor to the bank of elevators and waited, watching the entrance in the reflection of a mirror next to the first elevator. The elevator dispatcher was a man with thick glasses and a tight collar. He was tall, with shoulders stooped from years of working hard to look important. The elevator doors came open, and the dispatcher signaled his approval for the five waiting people to enter after three businessmen came out, but Karpo did not enter.

"This car up," he said to Karpo while the elevator waited and the young woman operating it watched in guarded curiosity lest she offend the militant dispatcher.

Karpo responded, turning to face the dispatcher, who mistakenly elected to attempt to stare him down. The crowd on the elevator grew impatient, and the operator continued to watch. It reminded her of two gunfighters she had seen in a Czech movie about American cowboys.

The sopping-wet stranger was the unblinking gunfighter. The dispatcher was the sheriff whose authority had been questioned, and Elena Soldatkin imagined herself the schoolteacher who would have to step in and make an emotional plea to stop the bloodshed, a plea that would have no effect in a film and that she would never make in reality, because the dispatcher was a most unpleasant man who was also the party organizer for the Ukraine Hotel. So she sat, watched, and tried not to show emotion, but at this she was an amateur compared to the strange, besoaked, pale skeleton of a man.

Suddenly, the pale man glanced toward her, looked at the mirror beside the elevator, and then entered the elevator, room being quickly created for him by the retreating figures, who wanted neither the moisture nor the aura he carried. The dispatcher, feeling quite triumphant, though a bit unsettled by the strange man, watched the elevator doors close and turned to gather his next flock for the next ascent. The massive woman carrying some kind of instrument case strode wetly toward him, and he calculated how many people could reasonably be allowed to occupy the same elevator with her, but he was certain it was a task he could handle with his usual expertise.

Two men in the rear of the elevator spoke in a whisper as Karpo's elevator moved slowly upward. They were not from Moscow. Their accents were from the west, possibly as far as Kiev.

"Because if we go to the Berlin," said one man with exasperation, "he'll bloat, get drunk. We'll get no business done."

"So we'll get no business done," the other man countered in a high voice, "But we'll get goodwill, and tomorrow they will owe us. Don't be impatient."

The two men got out at the sixteenth floor. By the eighteenth floor no one was left but Karpo and the operator. Elena said, "Floor," recalling that the dispatcher had never extracted a destination from the man. Elena had the sudden chill feeling that the man might pull out something he was hiding in his sling and plunge it through her back. Her voice was high, quivering slightly.

"Top," he said.

"Twenty," she answered, and threw the lever as far to

the right as it would go, knowing that there was no way to make the elevator move faster but willing it to do so. The elevator stopped with a jerk, and she reached over to throw the door open. Only then did she look back at the man, who said, "The roof. How do I get to the roof?"

Elena knew she should ask a question, challenge his authority, demand an explanation, but this was not a man one asked for explanations. It was a man you got out of your elevator and forgot as soon as possible. Elena was twenty-six years old and looked forward to twenty-seven and thousands of miles going up and down in the elevator and the movie she was going to see that night with her friend Nora.

"To the right, end of the corridor, There's a stairway, but I don't know if—"

The stiff man was already heading down the hall, his back to her, his secret protected by his hand, plunged into his wet sling. Elena closed the door without finishing her sentence. She planned to forget the encounter, at least till she could see Nora and build it into something more than it had been.

Karpo found the door without trouble. It was unmarked and unnumbered. He turned the handle and pushed. The heavy door gave way slowly. Had he been able to use his right hand, he could have—but he stopped that thought. One used what one had, overcame obstacles, did not weep when they appeared. He pushed the door open, went in, and moved up the concrete steps in near darkness.

There was a single light on the landing above. The light was a dull yellow and made his hand look jaundiced. The steps were clean and rough. On the floor above twenty, Karpo found himself in front of a metal door with a push bar. He pressed against it and stepped out onto the roof of the Ukraine. The wind slapped him and cracked the metal door closed with a clang. The rain had dwindled but not stopped. It pelted down on the flat pebbled roof, sending up an odor of strong warm tar that Karpo savored without quite making the sensation conscious. Above him for nine floors stood the front tower of the hotel with a star on its uppermost spire. He looked around, up, saw nothing, and heard only the rain brushing the roof and the slight wind.

There were turrets, outcroppings for air, heating, and simple decoration, many places to hide and wait, but no place to keep dry. Karpo did not expect to be there long. He strode to the edge of the building and looked over the low stone wall down at the bridge, the Moscow River, the city where he had spent his life. He felt himself merge with the building, could imagine himself disappearing, to be absorbed in the stone and the water. Perhaps he was a bit tired. If Colonel Snitkonoy were not a fool, an armed man would be up there now, but, Karpo decided, perhaps it was better this way.

He walked to a stone heating turret, stepped behind it, out of the line of vision of the door through which he had come, and demanded that his body ignore the throbbing, electric tingling in his right arm. He looked through the thinning rain at the modern building of the Council for Mutual Economic Assistance and the Mir (Peace) Hotel and let his breath take in the smell of his own humid sweat.

He heard the sound of someone coming before the door opened. When it did open with a loud clank, Karpo was standing well back, where he could see but not be seen.

It was the large woman in the dark flowered dress. She looked like a ripe country melon, the kind his mother had purchased once or twice when he was a child. The thought in this circumstance led Karpo to reach up and touch his forehead, which confirmed what he suspected. He was feverish. His body was damaged, and his mind was not at its best. He came as close to smiling as was possible for him, but no one, with the possible exception of Rostnikov, would have detected it had they been with him.

The woman trudged forward toward the edge of the hotel roof, stopped, took a small bottle out of her pocket, removed some green pills, and threw them into her mouth. Then she turned her head upward to the sky to take in rain to wash down the pills. The rain hit her face, pushing her hair from her eyes and mouth, and for an instant Karpo thought there was the remnant of something in the woman's face, something that might have been but had been burned away.

Her head came down, and she stood, arms folded at the edge of the building, looking down, waiting. They both waited for perhaps ten minutes, sharing the solitude. Then the rain began to ease, and within a minute it stopped. Behind him, Karpo could hear a bird singing as the woman knelt with some pain and opened her trombone case.

He waited till she lifted the rifle out, waited till she carefully loaded it, waited till she propped it up on the stone facade and looked down at the street, before he stepped out from behind the turret.

"No," he said as the bird sailed past him, singing.

The woman was not startled. In fact, for an instant Karpo thought that she might not have heard him, that she might be hard of hearing or so preoccupied that his word did not penetrate her consciousness. Then she turned to him, and he could see her strange smile of satisfaction. The rifle in her hands, large and clumsy, came around in her large hands and aimed at him, smelled him out. Karpo stopped no more than a dozen feet from her.

"You are a policeman," she said. It wasn't a question.

"I am a policeman," Karpo agreed. "Assistant Inspector Emil Karpo of the procurator's office. And you are—"

"A killer of policemen," Vera said with defiance.

"Yes, what is the name of this killer of policemen?"

"Vera Shepovik," she said, spitting out her own name with what sounded like hatred. "I don't mind telling you. I'm going to kill you. I saw you following me. I hoped you would be here. I was afraid you wouldn't. I—"

"I saw you compete in the university games three years ago," he said. "At the Palace of Sports in Luzhniki. Javelin and—"

"Hammer," she said. "I placed second in the hammer. That was my last competition."

"You were very good," he said. Karpo had no passion for sports, for athletic competition, but he did find satisfaction in the vision of athletes, Soviet athletes, who disciplined their bodies, drove them. It was something he respected, and so when Rostnikov had invited him to watch the competition, Karpo had agreed. Rostnikov had shown little interest in anything but the weightlifting, during which he talked constantly, pointing out nuances and tensions that Karpo could not discern.

"Do you want to know why it was my last competition?" she asked.

Karpo nodded.

"Because I discovered that I was ill, that I was poisoned, that steroids were eating away my organs from within." She took one hand off the rifle to touch her stomach, to indicate where the process of decay was taking place. "They used me; the great Soviet state used my body, used me like a zombie, and then cast me aside to die without meaning when their experiment failed."

Her hand went back to the rifle.

"And you are sure your illness was a result of—"

"I'm sure," she shouted. "I feel it."

"A doctor confirmed—"

"I don't need a doctor to confirm what my body knows," she said. "My mind knows that the state killed me and left my body to walk about. I know you are one of the tentacles of the state, that I must cut down as many tentacles as I can. My life may be small, but it will have this meaning, demand this attention. I'm dying."

"And so are we all," Karpo said, stepping a bit closer to the woman, whose red eyes were fixed on his own.

"But some of us sooner than others," she said with a smile.

"Yes," he agreed.

She raised the rifle, and Karpo saw the dark hole of the barrel searching his face. His chance was to keep her sights high, to move low after she shot. If the rifle came down, it would be aimed at his body, and even a miss might take off his head.

"Why aren't you afraid, policeman? There is a gun in your face. People with guns in their faces are afraid. People are afraid to die, policeman."

"You are afraid to die, Vera Shepovik." He took a step

forward and continued. "You are quite right. I am a part of the state. I can be killed, and you will either be caught or you will die from whatever it is that tears at you."

"Be afraid," she shouted. "It doesn't have meaning if you aren't afraid. It doesn't count if I can't see—"

"The policeman you shot two days ago was thirty years old," he said, moving to within four feet of her; the rifle was almost touching his mouth. "He was quite brave, a hero."

"And that is why you hate me," she said in triumph. "Now I understand. You want revenge."

"No. I want you to understand that your act has no meaning. You kill us, and there are others. You accomplish nothing. Come from this roof and we will get you to a hospital where you can be looked at, where you can find out what is really within you."

She laughed and looked for an instant at the sky, but the rifle did not move.

"And I will be kept alive long enough to be executed."

There was no denying it.

"I can't allow you to kill again," he said softly.

"And I can't stop," she said almost softly. "There is a painting in the Pushkin Museum. . . ."

The movement was strange, intimate, and Karpo, blaming his fever, his pain, the quivering cold, wet skin, felt that he could love this woman. The thought almost got him killed. The metal click of the rifle entered him, was absorbed without thought. When the bullet cracked, his head was already moving down to the right. There was a roar, an explosion, and he felt his inner ear vibrate and go deaf. His left arm went up, hitting the barrel of the rifle as he sprawled backward, awkwardly unable to use either hand to stop him from crashing to the rough, wet roof. He rolled quickly over, sensing the barrel of the rifle striking the space where his head had been.

Karpo scrambled up, expecting to be hit or pushed over the edge twenty floors to the street. He wondered what the sensation would be, whether he would have time to think, observe, before he was absorbed into the pavement.

He managed to get his pistol out awkwardly in his left hand as Vera raised the rifle to strike again.

"Enough," he said gently. "Enough."

Something in his voice stopped her. She had expected anger, hatred, but this walking death of a man gave her only a sense of understanding. It was not what it should be.

"Damn you, policeman," she said.

She threw the rifle over his head, and it sailed down toward Kutuzov Avenue.

"All over," Karpo said, feeling his head go light, warning him that he might soon simply pass out.

"No," she said, stepping to her right to the edge of the hotel. She looked over the side in the direction she had thrown her rifle. Her hair blew back. Tears were in her eyes.

"Perhaps, if I aim carefully, I can hit a policeman walking by. On the television they jump from airplanes and guide themselves." She looked down, and Karpo aimed his pistol at a pink, faded rose on her dress.

"No," he commanded.

She was standing on the narrow wall, not looking at him, looking downward, biting her lower lip.

"Vera," he said gently, and she looked at him. He had the impression that she was listening, was considering stepping back.

She did indeed say, "Maybe," as her foot slipped on the wet mounting and she went over the edge, her head striking the wall with a horrible crack before she tumbled out of Karpo's sight.

Karpo fell to his knees and managed to roll over to the trombone case, to pull it to him. He put his pistol back in its holster and laid his head on the case, his eyes to the gray sky. Emil Karpo passed out.

Lydia Tkach's hearing was poor. She resisted the urgings of her son and daughter-in-law to get an electric thing to stick in her ears. At the Ministry of Information Building where she worked filing papers, she was not a popular woman. The primary reason for her lack of popularity was that she called attention to herself by the volume of her conversation. She would, in addition, when able to trap a listener, be sure to get in the information that her son was a high-ranking government official. And so people avoided Lydia Tkach, which made her lonely and crotchety, which in turn made her turn her son and daughter-in-law into a captive audience at home.

"Something's wrong," she shouted with satisfaction when Sasha tried to enter the small apartment without calling attention to himself.

"Nothing's wrong," he answered, looking around for Maya. "Mother, I'm just tired."

"You look tired," Lydia shouted. "You look tired and dirty."

"Mother . . ." he said in a loud whisper.

"What have you been doing?"

"My job," he said, taking off his jacket and looking at the closed door of the bedroom, slightly more than closet-sized, that his mother slept in and in which Maya sometimes sought refuge after her long day of work. "Is Maya home?"

"Resting," Lydia shouted, holding up a finger to her lips to indicate that they should both be quiet, which was exactly what they were not being. "She's going to have a baby."

"I am well aware of that, mother," he said, brushing his hair back from his forehead. He wanted to look in a mirror to see if guilt were on his face. Sasha was very good at lying with his face, with his eyes. He had learned to develop it in his work. It was a skill that went well with his youthful, open face, but Marina, the car thief, had seen through it and through him, and now he moved to the table near the window with no place to hide.

"We're having dinner," his mother yelled, a knowing smile on her face. She was a frail woman with an iron will under which Sasha had frequently been broken. Lydia had never been physical, never hit him. She simply kept up her barrage of words and fierce determination until she achieved victory or drove her opponent from the room.

"We usually do, mother," he said, his stomach growling, wondering how he could face his pregnant wife.

"For dinner we're having kulebiaka stuffed with salmon and cabbage soup," she said, walking over to him. She was wearing her at-home sack, a simple baglike creation with three holes, one for the head and two for her arms. Lydia claimed it was the fashion in France to wear such things. Neither Sasha nor Maya had argued with her.

"And you want to know what else?"

"What else?" he asked dutifully, wanting to put his head in his hands, wanting to take a shower, wanting to emigrate to Albania.

"Cherry vodka, a whole bottle," Lydia said, putting her hands on her hips and waiting. Obviously, there was a question to be asked by her son, but he was too distracted to know what it might be.

Sasha loved his mother, truly loved her, but it was his dream to create some space between himself and her. With the baby coming, Maya was getting increasingly annoyed with the older woman. There was no room to get away after a hard day of work, and there would be less room when the baby came. It had been agreed, primarily by Lydia, that when the baby came, she would stop working and take care of it as soon as Maya was prepared to go back to work. Sasha and Maya had reluctantly agreed. There really was no choice.

"Do you want to know what we are celebrating?" she finally said.

Grateful for the help, Sasha said dutifully, "What are we celebrating?" He looked about for the bottle of cherry vodka so he could start the celebration.

"Guess. If you don't feel well enough to guess, I can understand."

"I'll guess." He sighed, sure that their conversation had roused the napping Maya. "I'll guess."

"Then guess."

"I'm trying," he said. The idea came to him quite madly that they were celebrating his moment of infidelity with Marina, that Maya had heard about it, had left, and Lydia had been so struck with joy at her daughter-in-law's departure that she had prepared a feast. But that made no sense. She stood waiting over him, about to shout.

"The baby," he said.

"We celebrate the baby when we get the baby," she said impatiently. "Don't be stupid. You're a smart boy."

"Ah . . . you're moving in with Aunt Valentina. Uncle Kolya died, and you're moving—"

"That would be something to celebrate? What's wrong with you?" She reached over and slapped the back of his head. "What's wrong with you? You look like you—Did you shoot somebody again? Like last time? You shot somebody."

He got up from the table and began to search in the small cupboard for the bottle of vodka. He found it, grabbed a glass, and turned back to the table, glancing out the window at the steamy after-rain street below.

"I didn't shoot anybody. Nobody shot me. I haven't lost my job. I don't know what we are celebrating. For the love of reason, mother, let me breathe."

"You are a hopeless case, Sashkala. Sometimes you are a hopeless case. I'll tell you what we are going to celebrate."

He opened the bottle and poured himself a large glass of vodka.

"Without eating? You are going to drink like your father without eating?" She reached atop the tabletop refrigerator behind him and pulled down a loaf of bread as he began to drink. He accepted the torn handful of bread she handed him and bit off a hunk to follow the half glass he had just downed.

"We are celebrating, mother, remember? But what we are celebrating not only eludes me; it is beginning to fill me with indifference."

She pulled out the chair across from him, reached for the bottle, and poured herself a healthy glassful of vodka. Sasha noticed that she did not accompany it with bread, but he said nothing.

"We are—" she began.

"—going to have a new apartment." Maya's voice finished from behind him.

Sasha turned to face her, expecting his eyes to betray his feelings, wanting to shout out his guilt, ask for forgiveness. He did not really hear what she had said. He took her in, her dark eyes, her smile, her simple brown dress, and the clear small circle of her growing belly. Her eyes met his and noticed something. Her smile dropped for a part of a heartbeat and then came back.

"Sasha," she said, moving to him, "are you all right? Do you have a fever? Did you—?"

"He didn't shoot anyone," Lydia shouted, taking a drink of vodka.

"I'm all right," he said, trying to smile. "I—did you say something about an apartment?"

"Our application was approved." Maya beamed, taking his head in her hands. "I went down today."

"We went down today to the housing ministry," Lydia amended.

"In North Zmailova," Maya said excitedly. "Much bigger than here. One bedroom and a small extra room, big enough for a bed. Lydia can have it. We'll have our own room with the baby, and later he can go to sleep in the bedroom and we can move him into a bed in the living room. It's right near the metro station."

"I get a television," Lydia said.

"Look happy, Sasha," Maya said, examining his face.

He smiled, but she could see tears.

"He was always like that," Lydia said, reaching for the bread and tearing off a piece. Crumbs fell on her dress. She swiped them off. "Emotional. Like his father after a drink or two. An emotional policeman. You have to control your emotions if you are going to be a success. I told your father that. Did he listen?"

Sasha wasn't listening to his mother.

"Let's eat," Maya said softly.

The dinner went well, and Sasha, after the bottle was finished, determined to devote himself to being a good husband, a good son, a good father, and a good policeman.

A few minutes after making that solemn resolution to himself, he had some difficulty remembering just what it was he had resolved to do. He knew it involved his family and recalled, perhaps, that it had involved working to get his mother a television set.

Sasha was feeling much better when the telephone rang. They were still talking at the table when the sound of the phone cut through his heart.

"It's the phone," his mother said, looking suddenly pale. "It's for you. Who calls here but the police people? I'll get it."

He leaped up before she could reach the phone and managed to answer first. Maya looked at him with concern, and he smiled back at her.

It was Zelach.

"I can't find the chief inspector," Zelach said wearily.

"Why are you looking for him?"

"The list he wanted is ready, the list of American tourists in Moscow," Zelach said. "It was long, but the chief inspector said I should make a shorter list of older men, men over seventy-five. That list's not so long. And—"

"And you have this list?" Sasha said, trying to avoid Maya's penetrating, questioning eyes.

"I just said I had the list," Zelach said with irritation. "I want to go home now."

"Leave the list on my desk. I'll be right there."

"But—" Zelach began as Sasha hung up the phone.

"Emergency," he said apologetically. "I have to get back to the office."

"Now?" asked Lydia, picking at the crumbs of salmon. "It can't wait till morning?"

It could certainly wait till morning, but Sasha wanted to get out, to control himself.

"No, it's an emergency, a murder."

He moved to Maya, giving her a quick kiss, and started to turn away, but she stood up and grabbed his sleeve.

"What?" he began.

"Whatever it is," she whispered, "try not to worry. Are you sick?"

"No," he said, sighing.

"Are you having trouble in your work?"

"A bit," he said, avoiding her eyes. "But it will pass."

"Touch the baby," she said, taking his hand. He touched her stomach. "Everything will be fine."

And, he thought, waving to his mother, perhaps it would.

To Rostnikov, the apartment building on Balaklava Prospekt looked that day like a child's gray building block. He had purchased a set of gray plastic blocks for Josef when his son was about seven, and Josef had rearranged his blocks into imaginative structures that he named "the typewriter without keys," "the radio with no sound," "the refrigerator with no doors," "the book with no pages," and "the ice cream van without wheels." This, thought Rostnikov, is the apartment without a mouth. It was a thought that depressed him as he slowly climbed the three flights of stairs toward the apartment of Sofiya and Lev Savitskaya. It depressed him because his own apartment on Krasikov Street was so much like it.

Going there was a risk, a slight risk, but a risk nonetheless. He had been officially ordered off the case. Were he to be caught, he could, would, simply say that he was informing those involved, the survivors of the victim, that the investigation would continue under another investigator when time permitted. He would argue, explain, that he was tying up loose ends to keep concerned citizens from lodging protests. The argument would be an absurd one. No one would pay attention to a protest from a distraught Jew whose old father had been murdered, but what could they do to Rostnikov? Take his job? If they wanted to dismiss him from his work, they would simply do it. Rostnikov had no illusions. He would continue to work as long as he continued to have a function that no one else could fulfill.

He ground his teeth as he arrived at the third floor and reached down to rub his complaining left leg. He had stopped home briefly to change into his other suit and to lay out his torn jacket neatly with a note to Sarah asking her please to repair it. The note had been carefully worded, brief but examined, to ensure that no word or phrase could give offense. Sarah's disappointment at their failure to get out of the Soviet Union had been great. At first she had seemed to accept it as inevitable. She took it like a Russian, but as the days passed and she became aware that an occasional KGB man would inquire about her at her work or she thought about the consequences of their failure to obtain permission to emigrate, consequences more for their son Josef than for themselves, she had begun to brood. The brooding got worse when she was dismissed without reason from her job at the music shop. Brooding didn't become her. She was normally cheerful, open, supportive. Brooding was Porfiry Petrovich's speciality. A small apartment could not sustain two brooders without the possibility of explosion.

Rostnikov had not called ahead that he was coming. There was no one to call. The Savitskayas had no telephone. Few Russians had telephones. The latest estimate was that in the entire Soviet Union there were no more than 20 million phones compared to more than 140 million in the United States. It was, therefore, a calculated risk to come to the Savitskaya apartment. The woman was a schoolteacher and the boy a student. They might well be home late in the afternoon. It had also struck Rostnikov that Sofiya Savitskaya was not the most social of citizens. As it was, he was proved right. He knocked once, solidly, on the apartment door and was greeted by a dreamy "Who is there?"

"Inspector Rostnikov," he said, and waited while she came to the door and opened it just enough to see him, a pointless protection, since he could simply push it open.

"What?" she said, one brown eye showing, puzzled and frightened, through the crack.

"I would like to come in and talk," he said. "What I have to say need not be shared by the neighbors."

She hesitated and then opened the door for him to enter. She waited till he was all the way in before closing the door. The apartment was hot, moist and hot, in spite of the open window. There was no draft, no opening for the breeze, should one arise, to seek out and enter.

She stood near the door, and he could see over her right shoulder the space from which the photo had been taken. There was something of the fragile bird about the woman that touched Rostnikov, though she was not thin. In fact, she seemed a bemused, disheveled, slightly younger version of his own Sarah, but that might simply be the cautious Jewishness of both women. There was no clear physical characteristic that marked Soviet Jews from other Russians. But there was a look nurtured by hundreds of years of wariness in an always-hostile culture.

"I would like a drink of water," he said gently.

"A drink of water," she repeated, as if no command could be acted upon unless programmed through her own voice. She moved, limped, to the small sink, turned on the faucet, and filled a glass for him. Instead of advancing to give it to him, she stood at the sink, holding it out. Rostnikov nodded solemnly and walked over to take it.

She was not pretty, he decided, looking at her as he drank, but there was that air of Cassandra, a distance, a sense that she was listening to voices on another plane. Rostnikov admitted that there was something intriguing about that, something that attracted him. Her air suggested madness, and madness suggested a vision he could not imagine, a fragile creative power that needed protection.

He drank the water and handed the glass back to her before he spoke.

"We have made some progress," he said.

She looked at him as if she had no idea what he was talking about.

"Progress in finding the killers of your father," he explained.

"It doesn't matter," she said, looking directly at him and making it quite clear that it didn't matter to her. "All I want is the photograph and the candlestick. Lev and I have very little to remember."

"When we catch the killers, we will have the candlestick. The killers do not have the photograph, however. We took that, as you may recall. And we will return it shortly.

"I have some names I want to say to you, names of the people who we think were in the photograph. I will say them, and you tell me if your father ever mentioned them, what he said. Can we do that?"

She didn't answer.

"And can we sit?"

She sat at one of the three wooden chairs at the small kitchen table, and he sat across from her. He considered asking for another glass of water just to keep his hands busy. Most Russians smoked. It was a habit Rostnikov had never considered.

"Mikhail Posniky, Lev Ostrovsky, Shmuel Prensky," he said. "I thought, perhaps, your brother Lev might be named for Ostrovsky, who was one of the men in the photograph."

"Never," she said without emotion.

"Your parents would never name—"

"Lev was named for my grandfather. But Mikhail Posniky—I heard that name. My father knew him, went to America with him. I think he died."

"And Shmuel Prensky?"

"The magic snake," she answered, looking down at her hands. "The poison snake of gold. To say his name is like saying the name of the Lord. It is forbidden."

"Your father said this?"

"In the dark, once or twice. At night. To my mother when she lived. Inspector, have you ever thought that being alive is very difficult?"

"I have thought this, yes."

"And?"

"And I eat my borscht, lift my weights, read my books, do my work."

"Do you have a wife and children?"

"A wife, a son, a grown son."

"You said your wife is Jewish. You said that the day my father was killed. Was it a lie?"

Their eyes met and Rostnikov smiled. "It was no lie."

"Shmuel Prensky is Jewish," she said almost to herself.

"So were all the men in the photograph," Rostnikov said in return, wanting to reach out and pat the nervous hand of the woman as it rested on the hard wood table. But he did not reach out.

She shrugged, dismissing the thought.

"Where is your brother?"

"At the home of a friend," she said. "He grew tired of all the police. All the questions."

"All the—You mean more policemen came to talk to you since I—since your father's death?"

Her head was shaking in confirmation.

"They came, asked these same questions. Came again. We can't move. Can't hide. We can only sit and answer. In life, no one ever came to see father. Now that he is dead, he has many visitors. Do you think it is hot in here?"

"It is hot," Rostnikov agreed. "I must go."

He could tell her now that the investigation was closed. It wasn't too late. What could she do? Could she cry, wail? This was a woman with dreaded dreams who wanted her candlestick, her photograph, and a reason for insanity.

Rostnikov stood up with the help of the table, because, as usual, his leg had begun to stiffen. Sofiya watched and, he noticed, rubbed her own crippled leg. As he moved to the door, she rose, took a step toward him, and looked up at his face with a question. He opened his arms, and she put her head on his chest. He held her, patted her head, and waited for her to weep. He felt her cheek against his shoulder, her breasts against his chest, and wondered how long it had been since anyone had held and comforted Sofiya Savitskaya. He wondered, in fact, if she had ever been held and comforted, and inside himself he wept for her.

They stood that way for several minutes, and she was so silent that Rostnikov thought she might have fallen asleep. He could feel her breathing against him.

"I must go," he said gently, but she didn't move back. He took her arms and held her a few inches away as he repeated, "I must go," and then he sat her in the kitchen chair. Her eyes were closed, and her shoulders remained close together as if she had been hypnotized.

"I will come back when I know more," he promised, going to the door. The woman did not move. He went out and closed the door noiselessly behind him. Then he paused to listen. If she cried, he might go back, invite her for dinner, stay with her and tell his life story, spin a tale about Isola in America, about Ed McBain's world of police who caught criminals and knew nothing of politics, of police who were supported by their system, policemen named Carella, Meyer, Kling, and Brown, of policemen in a nightmare world but one in which they could comfort each other and those they encountered who were the victims of the madness.

Rostnikov went home. He wondered when he looked up at the evening sun if Sofiya Savitskaya would remain in that chair, her shoulders together, her eyes closed, until a prince came who would break the spell. Rostnikov felt the grit and sweat under his rapidly wilting collar and knew he was no prince. He was, at best, a comic knight or a guardian of the secret, but he was no prince.

He almost wandered into a hole in the street clearly marked with a sign indicating *remont*, or repair, and he put off going home by entering a bakery where the line to find out the price was reasonably short. He got the price and then went to the line to pay the cashier. Ten minutes later he had gone through the third line, the one to pick up the bread, and was on his way home.

"Let's go to a movie," he growled when he finally returned to his apartment and saw Sarah, her red hair tied back, her face solemn, her dress dark, placing food on the table.

She stopped, looked at him with her hands on her hips, and cocked her head to one side, which reminded him of the way she had looked one afternoon in 1962 when he had teased her about going on a vacation. He remembered that it was 1962, because he had just finished the investigation of the murder of the three shoestore clerks on Lenin Prospekt, and he had been feeling wonderful.

"The Mir has a French movie about Napoleon and Josephine," she said, testing him, for she knew that Porfiry

Petrovich Rostnikov's taste went to action films and comedies.

"The Mir sounds perfect," he said, putting his bread on the table.

"Maybe, we could find—" Sarah began, ready to concede some ground.

"The Mir it shall be," he said. "We will eat after I lift my iron babies. I will wash, and we will lose ourselves in decadent history and French romanticism. You smile? Does that mean we shall hold hands and kiss in the darkness like children?"

"You were never a child, Porfiry Petrovich," she said, checking something cooking that smelled sweet and indefinable to Rostnikov, who had begun to remove his clothes and prepare himself for his beloved weights. It would, he decided, be a perfect night. He would merge with the weights, sweat upon his own sweat, exhaust himself, and eat. He would eat as if he were in a terrible contest in which he had to extract all taste and savor all odors to win. Then he would go with Sarah to the French movie and love it, talk about it, imagine himself Napoleon. For one night he would not be in Moscow. One night. That was all he could do, and deep down he thought that was all he really wanted to do.

EIGHT

EMIL KARPO OPENED HIS EYES, EXPECTING TO SEE THE gray sky above the roof of the Ukraine Hotel. Instead, he saw pale gray walls, the solid, unsmiling face of Porfiry Petrovich Rostnikov, and he heard voices around him.

"I saw a French movie last night," Rostnikov said, looking down at him. "The French laugh too much, with too little feeling and with almost no reason. Do you agree?"

"I'm not an expert of the French mentality," Karpo croaked through his painfully dry throat. He realized now that he was in a bed, in a hospital.

A man was standing beside the chief inspector. He was about forty with a birdlike chest and glasses with wire rims that made him look like an intellectual from a 1930s movie about the Revolution.

"The woman who fell from the roof," Rostnikov said. "She was the Weeper?"

Karpo nodded.

"This is Monday morning," Rostnikov said. "I'm going to sit on your bed." He did. "They didn't call me yesterday when it happened. I think it was Procurator Khabolov's way of punishing me for the destruction of his Chaika. Well, you are supposed to be curious. You are supposed to be amused. You are supposed to be burning with curiosity about this destroyed Chaika, and you just lie there."

"Comrade inspector," Karpo whispered painfully, "I

have neither a sense of humor nor a morbid curiosity about the humiliation of others."

"See?" said Rostnikov, turning to the man with the glasses. "Didn't I tell you he would steal his way into your heart, Alex?"

"You told me he would steal his way into my heart," Alex agreed, moving forward to Emil Karpo's side and looking down at him intently.

"She jumped," Karpo said, his eyes on those of Rostnikov's companion. "I will detail it in my report. Did she injure anyone in her fall?"

"No, no one, though the street had to be closed off for almost half an hour, I understand. The rifle she had with her went through the window of a clothing shop."

Karpo took in the six other patients in the ward room. None had a visitor; three were displaying mild curiosity about Karpo and his guests, and three were in no condition to respond to their environment.

The man named Alex put his hand on Karpo's forehead, leaned down to look into his eyes, and then reached for the numb right arm.

"Comrade inspector, I take it this man is some kind of health professional and not a morbid lunatic you encountered in the hall," Karpo said, watching his arm being lifted, seeing the dingy gray sleeve of his gown slide back, feeling a tingling in the fingers as the man examined.

"See, Alex, I told you he had a sense of humor. He can deny it all he likes, but Emil Karpo could make a living as a comedian."

"He is very funny," Alex agreed blankly as he ran his hand over the limp arm and bent it at the elbow.

"Alex is a doctor," Rostnikov whispered, "but we will keep that a secret. The woman who is supposed to be your physician would not take consultation with exuberance. Alex is my wife's cousin. Remember? He went to a real doctor's school in Poland."

Alex prodded away, ignoring Rostnikov, who continued, "On the way in we stopped at the X-ray department and told a slight lie which enabled Alex to examine your X-rays."

"They were botched." Alex sighed, working ahead. "But I could see enough. I just want to be sure..." He rolled Karpo's shoulder firmly and caused a pain that brought a minor grimace to Karpo's pale face.

"You are supposed to give vent to some feeling when you have pain," Alex said, looking at Karpo's pale face. "How am I supposed to know I'm hurting you if you do not cooperate?"

"I will scream the next time," Karpo said.

"Would you like some water? They stuck a tube down your nose, but I don't know what the hell for," Alex said, shaking his head and reaching for the water glass on the small table. "These sheets aren't even properly cleaned."

Karpo took a drink of water, a small sip that burned as it rolled over inflamed and tender nodules at the base of his tongue.

"I'm going to tell you what you should do," Alex said, adjusting his little black tie professionally. The room was warm, but a breeze did flow through the open windows. A spot of sweat showed, clearly etched like the outline of an amoeba on Alex's white shirt. "You should get out of here as fast as you can. Tell them you feel fine before they operate on you and maim you for life or, worse, infect you in an unsterile environment. They are controlling your fever with drugs. Who knows what drugs. Do you know why you have a fever?"

"I—" began Karpo, but Alex ignored him.

"You have a fever because you have an infection in your shoulder resulting from an improperly reset dislocation. You also have a severe cold. You can recover from the cold at home after I reset your arm in my office."

"Listen to him, Emil Karpo," Rostnikov whispered.

"Here you get treated free," Alex said, adjusting his glasses. "A service of the state. I'll treat you for two hundred rubles. That's a month's salary for the doctors who work in this hospital, and as you probably know, it is less than a factory worker makes, which explains something about the quality of care you get here."

"The system will eventually operate if corruption is controlled and the people accept the sacrifices necessary," Karpo croaked.

Alex turned to Rostnikov with a shrug. "You ask me to see the man, and I get quotes from Lenin and insults. When I was in medical school in Poland, we had a regular underground railroad of your Soviet sacrificers in high places shipping themselves and their families West for real medical treatment. The head of the Soviet Academy of Sciences, Keldysh, got an American doctor when he had heart trouble."

"I'm sorry, doctor," Karpo said. "Then why do you stay in the Soviet Union if you feel this way?"

Alex shook his head at the density of some people and leaned over to breathe on Karpo and examine his face through the thick glasses.

"They won't let me go," he said. "No more quotas for Jews. No more doctors getting out. But you know what I really think. They want to keep us around for when they really need competence. There are little rooms full of Jewish doctors, Catholic writers, Mongol craftsmen, all of whom will be plucked out in emergencies or rot until one comes. Meanwhile, two hundred rubles is a small price to pay for the use of your arm."

"Pay him, Emil," Rostnikov said.

A man two beds away shouted, "Don't be a fool. You have two hundred rubles; pay him. If he could cure rotted lungs, I'd pay him five hundred rubles."

"See," said Rostnikov, "even the proletariat support this exception. You will violate no law, Emil, and you'd be doing me a favor. I'm getting tired of visiting you in hospitals every time you catch a criminal. There is something in you that seeks destruction."

"Not so loud," said Alex, pouring himself a drink of water from the nearby pitcher, examining it, and then deciding that it was too suspicious to drink. "The state frowns on any suggestion of neurosis. Everything is organic. Neurosis is decadent, something for the West Germans,

French, English, and Canadians. Don't drink any more of this water."

"I think he should be treated in the hospital," cried a man in the corner. "We have to stay here. The state takes care of us. He should stay here."

"Shut up, you old *nakhlebnik*, you parasite," said the man with the rotted lungs. "You'd pay a thousand rubles if you could get a new pair of balls."

"Gentlemen," Rostnikov said, standing because his leg would no longer permit him to sit. "There is merit to what you both say, but if you don't stop shouting, a doctor will come in."

"A doctor," said the man with the lung problem. "That would be a novelty."

"Capitalist traitor," coughed the man with no balls.

"Eunuch," countered the man with no lungs.

And then both fell silent.

"I'm going," said Alex. "I can hear this kind of talk at home. Porfiry Petrovich, tell him how to get to me if he decides he prefers going through life with two arms instead of one."

And off went Alex, leaving the two policemen alone.

"You'll do it?"

"I will see what the doctors here say," whispered Karpo. From the bed Karpo could not see the woman who had entered the ward as Alex was leaving, but Rostnikov watched her enter, look around, see them, and head in their direction. She was tall, perhaps in the late thirties, with billowing brown hair. Her face was not pretty in any conventional way, but it was handsome, strong. She strode with confidence, her green dress slightly tight, very Western.

"You are Chief Inspector Rostnikov?" she said, holding out her hand.

Rostnikov took it and nodded.

"I am Mathilde Verson," she said.

Karpo looked at her as did all the other patients in the room who were awake or capable, but Karpo was the only one who had seen her before. In fact, for seven years he had seen her regularly, every two weeks on Thursday afternoons for about an hour. He had also seen her occasionally to get information about other prostitutes who might be involved in or have information about some crime he was investigating. Karpo looked at her without betraying surprise but with a question.

"How did you know I—" he began, but Mathilde was looking at Rostnikov, and Karpo understood. He stopped the question and addressed a new one to the chief inspector. "How long have you known about Mathilde?"

"Who knows?" He shrugged, dismissing the question. "A few years. I'm a detective, remember? I know things. So what's so important about this? Did you think someone would blackmail you, discover you might be human and not just an efficient pawn of the state? It was refreshing to discover that you are a man like other men, Emil Karpo."

Talking was difficult for Karpo, but things had to be said. "We are all animals," he said dryly. "We cannot deny our animalness. We must acknowledge, channel, and control it so we can carry out our duty."

"Can you believe it, chief inspector?" Mathilde Verson said, sitting on the bed. "He is always this romantic. Am I here for pay, Karpo? Do you think I came here to do business? There's a performance of *Swan Lake* at the Bolshoi this afternoon. That's four intermissions. You know how many tourists I could line up today? I'm giving up as much as one hundred dollars in American money by coming to see you. You know how Americans spend rubles? They think they're play money, little dollars with funny pictures of Lenin on them."

"I'm moved by your sacrifice," Karpo muttered.

Mathilde looked to Rostnikov for support. He gave her a shrug and adjusted his jacket to show that he was about to leave.

"The chief inspector said you might enjoy a visitor," she said to Karpo. "I'll just sit here a few minutes, exude personality, and have you smiling before you control yourself. You believe that?"

"I do not smile," Karpo whispered seriously.

"I'm going," Rostnikov said. "See if you can convince him."

"What's all this?" bellowed a woman in a white coat, striding toward them, a black file folder under her arm. She was of no known age. Her size was small, her hair was pulled back tightly, and she wanted control.

"Visitors," said Rostnikov.

The woman eyed Mathilde, appeared to discern her profession, and turned to Karpo.

"They are parasites," shouted the man with no balls.

"Hah," croaked the lungless one. "You can't even keep your insults straight. You are the parasite."

"Quiet," shouted the woman. She turned to Karpo, and Rostnikov hesitated so he could listen. "You are awake."

"I am awake," agreed Karpo.

"I am Doctor Komiakov," she said, opening the worn, dark folder and examining it. "I'm afraid I have some difficult news for you. Your right arm is infected and will have to be removed. I would rather not be so abrupt with this information, but you must know that the situation is severe, and you are a police officer. The surgery will be performed sometime tomorrow, and you should be functioning several weeks after that. There is even the possibility of a prosthetic device. Do you have a question?"

"Yes," said Karpo, trying to sit up. His head was light, and he felt dizzy. He realized that the first touches of an aura indicating a migraine might be on him. "How do I get my clothes?"

The doctor looked at Rostnikov, who offered her no support, so that she had to turn to Mathilde, who smiled.

"You are a very sick man," the doctor said.

Karpo was up now, his feet dangling over the side of the bed.

"My clothes," he repeated.

Outnumbered, the doctor closed her notebook with a slap. "That is your right as a citizen," she said grimly. "But I warn you that the infection is almost certain to kill you. You'll have to sign papers indicating that you chose to leave the hospital in spite of my warnings."

Mathilde held out a hand to help Karpo, who had managed to retain his dignity in spite of the absurd hospital gown. At first he rejected her offered hand and then took it.

The two debating patients behind them argued at a somewhat lower level the relative merits of leaving the hospital.

"It may take a while to get your clothes," Rostnikov observed. "I'll wait."

But as it turned out, he could not wait. After five minutes, Sasha Tkach entered the ward, looked around, spotted Rostnikov, and hurried over.

"Karpo," he said, brushing his straight hair back from his forehead. "How are you?"

"He is well, fine. We are waiting for his pants," said Rostnikov. He didn't introduce Mathilde, though Tkach stood waiting for an introduction. "Why are you here?"

"Posniky," he said with a smile. "We found him. He's a guest at the Metropole Hotel. He has a plane ticket to New York for this evening. I left Zelach to watch him. He's with a younger man."

"No one approached them?"

Tkach couldn't stop looking at the woman helping Emil Karpo to stand, but he tried not to look at her, to wonder. Karpo had always been a puzzle to him, a person to stay away from unless they were forced together for an investigation. Emil Karpo and this woman did not fit together.

"No one approached them. They don't know they have been identified, are being watched."

"Good, fine," Rostnikov said, sighing. "Then you and I will drive to the Metropole for a little drink. Emil, Comrade Verson, you are on your own. I'll give you Alex's address this evening."

Emil Karpo lifted his head to speak, realized there was nothing to say, and watched his two fellow officers of the state as they left the ward and the smell of alcohol behind them.

* * *

There was no real excuse for going to the Metropole. Rostnikov was off the case, had been told to stop the investigation. There was almost no way out of this if it came to a confrontation with Procurator Khabolov. His only hope was to bring in the killers, apologize for having them accidentally fall into his hands, and back away, taking the consequences. He could do one other thing. He could simply let Tkach turn them in and take no credit at all, simply disappear, but it was not in Porfiry Petrovich Rostnikov to disappear. He had tried it before and failed.

Tkach and Rostnikov rode in a bumpy taxi. It was hot all over Moscow, but a breeze through the open car window felt good. Rostnikov watched the streetlights go by and said nothing as they turned down Marx Prospekt.

"You want me to go with you to their room if they're in?" asked Tkach to the back of Rostnikov's head. "They are probably packing to leave."

Rostnikov grunted a barely audible no.

For the rest of the trip, Tkach was silent.

Rostnikov was quite familiar with the Metropole. He had investigated murders committed there, thefts, interviewed suspects.

There was an Old World seediness about the old hotel. One expected to encounter criminals in its dusty halls and shabby restaurant. The food was awful, the service terrible even by Moscow standards. Criminals of some stature were, however, almost obligated to make an appearance at the Metropole. On the staircase leading up to the mezzanine of the hotel stood a large bronze statue of two naked children passionately kissing. The statue symbolized the hotel and had become a good-luck charm for the bolder criminals who touched the eternally embracing underage couple.

Rostnikov liked the Metropole. It was like stepping into the past. He could, at least for a moment, imagine himself Dostoyevski's Porfiry Petrovich, for whom he was named, could imagine himself fencing verbally with a rapidly wilting Raskolnikov.

When the cab stopped, Tkach paid the driver, and Rostnikov moved ahead, not even glancing back across Sverdlov at the Bolshoi where, he knew, *Swan Lake* would soon be starting.

Zelach was seated conspicuously in the lobby, his hands folded on his lap, his eyes looking toward the entrance to the restaurant. He spotted Rostnikov and stood to greet him.

"They are in the restaurant," Zelach said.

"Fine."

"I'll point them out to you."

"I think I'll know who they are," said Rostnikov.

Tkach had now joined them. "Zelach, place yourself at the entrance of the restaurant," he said. "I don't care if they see you. In fact, it would be better if they do. Sasha, you make your way to the door by the kitchen. Just stand there looking like a policeman."

Tkach had no idea of how to look like what he was, but he nodded and watched Rostnikov move slowly, pulling his reluctant leg behind him. The several people in the lobby worked hard not to watch the scene, but watch they did.

As he entered the restaurant and let his eyes take in the various tables, he was grateful that the regular orchestra was not there. It was too early, but they were loud and terrible at any time. He did not want to shout over them.

There were a few dozen people in the room and at one table a man and woman Rostnikov recognized. The man had been imprisoned for beating another man who filled beer vending machines. The man pretended not to see the policeman.

Then Rostnikov saw the two men he was looking for. They were seated near the marble fountain in the center of the room in front of the stage, where there was no orchestra. The light from the fountain played on the stained-glass window behind the stage, and Rostnikov felt quite comfortable as he made his way to the two men and listened to the gentle splashing of the water in the fountain and the murmur of voices in the room.

The two men did not look up until he was standing next to the table. Even then only the younger of the two raised his head. The other man, the old man with the white hair, looked at his drink.

"Good afternoon," Rostnikov said amiably in English. "I am Chief Inspector Porfiry Petrovich Rostnikov. I do not know what name you are registered under, but you are Mikhail Posniky."

The younger man, a burly figure, very much the way Sofiya Savitskaya had described him, started to rise, his eyes looking about.

"Sit down, Martin," the old man said in English, taking a sip of his wine. "We're in the middle of Moscow. Where are we going to run to?"

"May I sit?" Rostnikov said, still in English. "I have a bad leg. The war."

"Sit," said Posniky in Russian, and Rostnikov sat. Rostnikov could see a faint resemblance between this old man and the young one in the photograph. This man's face was a dry landscape, a parched riverbed filled with crevices. "You like wine, chief inspector?"

"That would be nice."

Rostnikov glanced at the younger man, who was looking around the room. His eyes stopped first on Zelach, then circled and found Tkach. If he panicked, Rostnikov was prepared to reach out and grab him. He looked trained, formidable, possibly even a challenge. Posniky's very blue eyes came up and met Rostnikov's.

"Don't do anything stupid, Martin," the old man said in English.

"Thank you," said Rostnikov, accepting a glass of dark wine.

"The wine isn't as I remembered it," Posniky said, looking at the glass. "Has it changed that much, or have I?"

"It has changed," said Rostnikov. "But you've been gone for a long time. If you would feel more comfortable speaking English . . ."

"More than sixty years," Posniky said with a little smile. "I'll try Russian, though my phrases may be a bit out-of-date and there are many words I've forgotten. I am over eighty years old. Do I look it?"

"I would have guessed sixty," said Rostnikov, sipping the wine. It was awful.

"Let's try—" Martin said, leaning forward, his voice urgent.

"Sit and do what you are told," Posniky said with authority. Martin sat back and divided his attention between the three policemen in the room.

"The candlestick," Rostnikov said. "You have a story. I would like to hear it."

"I have a story," the old man said. "Do we have time?"

"We have time," said the detective, placing his half finished drink on the table.

"In 1891—" he began. "You'll forgive me if I go back that far. It might help you to understand the—how do you say, ugly?"

"*Nekrasivyi*," said Rostnikov.

"Ah, yes," said the old man, shaking his head at the memory of the word, "the ugly details. In the winter of 1891 the Gentile soldiers of the *fonie*, the czar, came to Yekteraslav for their quota of boys twelve and older who were to go for an indeterminate period, which the *fonie* forever varied from five to forty years. The longer the period of service, the more likely the boy to die or accept Christ, though Jewish boys had proved stubborn and deaths outnumbered conversions among Hebrew soldier children. It had been agreed that only one son would be taken for each family. According to my father, the Russian officer who came that day was a foolish man, a stupid man. He took who he wanted, which meant my father and his two brothers, one of whom was only eleven. My uncles died. My father came back in six years, half mad."

Rostnikov nodded to show that he was listening, but the old man was not watching the policeman. He was holding his wineglass in both hands and watching the last drops as he spoke more to himself.

"My father was arrested in 1909 by an officer who came to the door in a blue coat and fur hat. I was only a few years old, but I remember my father, or—who knows?—my mother may have described him so often that I think I remember him. He was arrested because we had a local shopkeeper's son working for us during the small harvest of our farm. The soldier at the door quoted the May Laws of 1881 stating that Jews could not hire Christian domestics without the express permission of the regional governor. The shopkeeper's son was only half Christian, and we paid him only with a few vegetables. We had no money, but"—Posniky shrugged—"they took my father, and we never saw him again. . . . My father, the village lunatic.

"And now," Posniky said, looking up with narrow eyes at the uneasy Martin, "and now ten years later, the Revolution. I was a boy. My friends were boys. Yekteraslav was an isolated Jewish village. We knew little of the Revolution. We didn't know which side was which. Some said the Jews would be better off after the Revolution. Most of us didn't believe it. Shmuel Prensky believed it. Abraham Savitskaya and I had lost too many relatives to the Christian Russia to believe it."

"And Ostrovsky," Rostnikov added, reaching for the bottle of wine. It was awful wine, but it was wine. "The actor."

Posniky looked up warily, not quite startled. "It will be easier to tell my story if you let me know what you know so I don't have to repeat—"

"I know names," Rostnikov said, biting back a bitter sip. "I know events of the last days, the murder of Abraham Savitskaya by you and your companion, the theft of the candlestick."

"It was no theft," the old man said with some emotion. "It was mine. It was my mother's. When the Reds came to our village in 1919 or 1920 to collect young men the way the *fonie* had collected our fathers, Abraham and I decided to get out. My mother and his gave us some food, and my mother gave me the candlestick. It was all she could give, and it was worth little. I said good-bye to my mother and sister, and we left on a winter morning. We were young, too stupid to see the uselessness of what we were trying, to get to Riga, to walk to Riga or steal a ride, but to get to Riga and get on a boat for Canada or America. We didn't know about passports. We didn't know that the few rubles in our pockets would buy not even enough bread for the trip. We assumed other Jews would help us on the way. We had names of friends of friends in towns along the way. We never found the towns or the friends. How much detail do you want, policeman?"

"As much as you wish to give," said Rostnikov, checking to see that Zelach and Tkach were alert. Zelach, across the room, looked puzzled by the scene.

"When we got to the road leading out of town," Posniky said, "we were too stupid even to go across the fields. We met two soldiers who had been left to stop just what we were doing. One was young. One was quite old. Their uniforms were makeshift, and they were surprised when we killed them. They expected docile young Jewish boys to run back into town, weeping. They had one horse between them, and both were standing on the ground, ordering us to turn around, when I pulled out the brass candlestick from my cloth sack and hit the young one in the face. His cheek gave way, and he tried to scream. I hit him again while the old soldier watched. Neither of them were real soldiers. The old one turned to run, but Abraham leaped on him, and I beat him to death, too. Since then, I have killed others."

"Including Abraham Savitskaya," said Rostnikov.

Martin was examining the faces of the two men across from him, trying to understand odd words in a foreign language, tense with frustration. Rostnikov was sure the young man would have to be dealt with before the afternoon was over.

"Including Savitskaya," agreed Posniky. "We dragged the bodies into the gray weeds off the road, and we ran through the field, leaving the horse standing in the middle of the road. Neither of us even considered taking the horse."

"Young boys often do very foolish things," said Rostnikov.

"And old men," added Posniky, holding up his glass, which Rostnikov refilled with wine.

"Mr. Parker," Martin said, glancing at Rostnikov. "I think—"

Posniky didn't even bother to look at the man. He shook his head and held up a wrinkled hand to quiet him. And then he went on with his story, interrupted only by a waiter, who brought a fresh bottle of wine and some bread.

"The trees were thin in near spring, and they gave little protection in the light of day, so we had to walk deeper in the woods to be sure we weren't seen from the road. When we heard a cart passing, we found shelter and waited. By early evening we had circled around a pair of small villages and watched a line of men on horseback heading in the direction from which we had come.

" 'They're coming for us,' Abraham said softly.

" 'No,' I told him, rubbing my lower back and putting down my sack. 'They are riding slowly and laughing.'

" 'Why are we still hiding in the woods instead of walking the roads?'

" 'We will take no chances until we are far away.'

" 'And how will we get on a boat at Riga? We have no money.'

" 'When we get to Riga'—I sighed—'we will find the money.'

" 'God willing,' said Abraham.

"A savage cold rain hit by evening, driving us under an outcrop of rocks where children had been before us, leaving a few torn books and pieces of glass. We shared the last of our cheese, drank rainwater from our clothes, and slept chilled. I remember dreaming of a town I had never seen, a town with no people, a town where rows of houses were being torn down. I had to run from house to house to stay ahead of the men and machines that moved forward to knock down the walls and send the dust of brick and mud into the air. I fled to a river and a long bridge that frightened me. I trembled and hesitated to put my foot on the white bridge, but behind me I heard the breathing of a sick cow, and I put my foot forward just as I woke up.

"We moved slowly, so slowly that our feet sometimes sank ankle-deep into mud in the woods and fields. The roads were a bit better, but we still avoided them. Sometimes we saw or heard someone working in a field, and one time we moved boldly through a nameless town and asked a ragged water carrier if we were on the right road to Riga.

"'You're on the right road, but you'll both be old men by the time you walk there.' The water carrier was a dry old man himself, a stick of a man, a kindling of a man with a brittle beard and no teeth. Very much like Abraham Savitskaya was in the bathtub when Martin and I found him.

"'We haven't any money,' Abraham said.

"The old man opened his mouth to comment or laugh but said nothing. Instead, he held out his water bucket to us, and we took a drink. The street was cobbled, and three little children wearing sacks for clothes played near us, some game with sticks and a little ball. I thanked the old water carrier, and we hurried out of town and back off the road.

"After three days of travel, Abraham was shivering and estimated that we had gone no more than a tenth part of our journey at most. Even if we could keep up our present pace, it would be at least thirty days before we reached Riga, and Abraham, always fragile, could not keep it up for thirty days.

"'We can go back,' he said, sitting on a wet tree stump. 'We could hide in the fields until we're sure it's safe.'

"I remember searching my sack for the last of our bread, finding it and tearing it in two for us.

"'We killed two soldiers,' I reminded him. 'We will not be soon forgotten. And I don't want to go back. You can go back if you want to.'

"We sat in the darkness, hugging ourselves, waiting for the night cold to take us. Abraham was first to give in to the chill and let it carry him to sleep, but I fought it, gritted my teeth, challenged until I felt I had proven myself and could allow my body the reward of rest. Before I slept, however, I planned.

"The next day's travel was like the last, and we spoke

little. The road turned, and we followed it, afraid that we had made a mistake and were now bound in the wrong direction, had somehow missed a turn and were headed into the vastness of an endless Russia toward Moscow; but the road gradually turned back in a direction I thought was north. Late in the brown afternoon we came to a large town and circled it. It took us an hour, and we never discovered the town's name.

"'We'll wait here,' I said. We were at the side of a road leading north from the town, and we sat in the woods about five hundred yards from the last house.

"'I can go no further, Mikhail,' Abraham said.

"'We'll go no further,' I said, pulling my mother's brass candlestick from my sack. I probably looked mad as the falling sun hit my face. Abraham backed away in fear and sat in silence.

"A few carts and wagons, and even an automobile, went by, away from the town, followed by a few people on foot, and then a rather elegant carriage went into the town. From behind a bush we watched them all as I held the brass candlestick tightly in the dark, dirty palm of my right hand. We looked at each other, two wild men, creatures of darkness, and in the midst of this meaninglessness I felt a power of nothing to lose.

"When the sun had almost disappeared across the wide field opposite us, a carriage clattered slowly from the town.

"'Now,' I said, rising, and Abraham rose, knowing what we would do without being told, transforming the deed into a ritual to allow us to do it, a pagan act born of despair as we two dark figures hurried forward, a brass candlestick in my hand, a stick in his.

"'On the road,' I said. 'Stop the carriage. Even if you have to kill the horse. Stop the carriage.' And I disappeared behind a ridge of low rocks.

"Abraham hurried forward, lumbered on legs turned stiff from sitting for hours, blood pumping to his throbbing head, probably thinking he might die before the deed was done, but he did not die. When the carriage with one horse turned the bend in the road, Abraham, a dark, spindly mantis, as much animal as man, stood in the road and frightened the gray horse. Had the driver urged him on, the horse would have run Abraham down and hurried into the coming night, but the driver, like the horse, was startled and stopped.

"The driver, a middle-aged man with a fine black coat and glasses, stood up and shouted something at Abraham, who reached up for the horse and held its muzzle. The angry man seemed frightened. I could see Abraham simply watch and wait as the man reached for something under the seat. Abraham strained his neck over the horse's head as he petted it to see what the man was doing. When the gun came out, Abraham did not look afraid, only curious. He was not even afraid when the man raised the weapon in his direction and sputtered something. He did not become afraid even when he saw me work my way around from behind the carriage. The bullet and my swing of the candlestick came at the same time. The bullet leaped into the darkness above Abraham's head, and he turned to watch it but saw nothing as the sudden night swallowed it. He had to pet and talk softly to the horse, whose eyes opened wide with fear at the sound of the struggle behind him.

"There was a rocking of the carriage and a terrible sound of something hard hitting bone, then a cry, not a cry really but a gasp that sounded like a child saying, 'Why?'

"'Hurry,' I whispered. 'Before someone comes by. Hurry.'

"Abraham hurried to the carriage and moved his head close to see the man, who lay slumped forward. Perhaps he expected blood, but could make nothing out in the darkness.

"'Quick,' I said, breathing quickly. 'Let's get him into the woods. Quick.'

"We lifted the man, and we could feel that he was still alive, though his right arm, the one that had held the gun, hung at an impossible angle, and we knew it was broken. When we had moved behind some rocks, we leaned over to listen to the man's chest.

"'He breathes,' I said softly.

"'A little,' said Abraham.

"'A little.'

"We hurried back to the carriage and drove into the night with me at the reins, feeling confidence returning for the first time since we had left Yekteraslav. I turned to share my feeling with Abraham, but he was slumped forward, his face in his hands.

"'You think he's dead?' asked Abraham, squinting into the darkness.

"'No,' I replied. 'He's not dead.'

"'How do you know?'

"'I don't know,' I cried. 'Stop talking.'

"We rode in silence and opened the cloth purse of the man we had robbed to find money, both paper and coin. It seemed like a lot.

"'We had to do it,' said Abraham.

"I nodded in the darkness, the wind and the smell of the sweating horse overwhelming me as I pushed the money in my pocket and flung the purse and the gun into the night. I did not want to know more about the man.

"'If they find him, when they find him, they will come looking for this carriage,' I said. 'We'll give ourselves a day with it. No more.'

"'It's a fine carriage and a fine horse,' said Abraham, sounding well to me for the first time since we left Yekteraslav.

"'Maybe we can sell it,' I said as I climbed into the back seat and lay down to rest. 'Do not stop in any town or village. I'll sleep an hour, and then we'll rest the horse and I'll drive.'

"Abraham agreed, though I knew he would have liked to drive the carriage forever, never stopping or thinking, just feeling the reins and the jogs in the road.

"I slept for four hours. When I awoke, the carriage had stopped. Abraham had unharnessed the horse and was letting it eat dry grass off the road. Across a marshy field, I could see a town that looked large, but it was much too soon for Riga.

"'Stay here with the horse,' I told Abraham. 'I'll go into the town and buy some clothes. Two ragged Jews riding a fine carriage is not going to be overlooked.'

"'So we will become two fine Jews with a carriage,' Abraham said with a smile.

"I nodded and looked at my friend, whose cap had slipped forward over his eyes, making him look like a village fool as he urged the horse to eat.

"'Talk to no one and stay here,' I said.

"'I will.'

"The town was Gomel, and the streets were cobbled, but there were still huge puddles from the thawing snow and rain. There were many Jews in their beards and hats. I could see the tips of their prayer shawls under their coats, but I needed no signs of clothing to recognize other Jews, with their dark, frightened look that marked them even if their features did not.

"A small boy with fingers sticking through ragged gloves sold me two hard bagels in the street from a woven straw basket. I ate one and put the other in my pocket for Abraham.

"'Where can I buy some clothes?" I asked the boy in Yiddish.

"The boy looked at me without looking, for to look openly might earn a blow, might imply that the stranger was too ragged to be looking for decent clothing. The boy could not have been more than nine, but he had learned much, perhaps all of what he would need for life in Gomel.

"'Nothing expensive, mind you,' I said. I knew a coin to the boy would get me a quick answer, but I was reluctant to part with the money. My plan was forming: we would spend no more than we had to, because I didn't know how much it might cost to get on a boat to England or America. In the near sleep of the night before I had decided that we had to get by on the money we had taken from the man with the gun, that if we did make it on the money, then the man would have made a contribution to our survival. The attack would have been necessary and meaningful, a sacrifice. Anything less than that and what we had done would be an act of brutality, meaningless animal brutality. The man would recover, get more money, buy another carriage. In fact, I had reasoned, this might turn out to be the best deed the man had ever done, to help two desperate young men.

"'. . . dead,' said the boy with the bagels.

"'Dead?' I cried, looking around.

"'I said,' continued the boy, 'that Menahcan the tailor is dead, but his son, Yigdol, has clothes. I'll take you.'

"I followed the boy for a few streets to a two-story brick building with a wooden door the boy pointed to and waited. I impulsively took out a coin and gave it to him.

"'*Shalom*,' said the boy.

"'*Shalom*,' I said, and knocked at the door.

"Yigdol the tailor proved to be a few years older than I, a few inches taller. There were no words or questions, just guarded looks of curiosity through the young tailor's thick glasses. Yigdol's one-room home and shop was small, one wall lined with cheap thin books, the other with heaps of clothing.

"'I need a suit,' I said.

"'Desperately,' said Yigdol, looking over his glasses. I wondered why he kept the room so dark, for it seemed obvious that a man who sews and reads in the dark would soon go blind, and Yigdol seemed well on the way to it.

"'You have something, something good, not work clothes but not too expensive? I have some money. Not much, but some.'

"Yigdol looked at me, put aside the dark cloth he was sewing, and went to a black pile in the corner near a dirty window. Outside a child was screaming at another child.

"In ten minutes, we had negotiated for a reworked suit and a white shirt, and only when the negotiation was completed did I mention the suit for Abraham, a suit that would have to be chosen without the wearer present. Yigdol acted as if he understood, and a second suit was selected.

"In preparation, I had shifted a small amount of money from one pocket to the next and took out a few crumpled rubles to pay the tailor, who looked at them and at me.

"'Is there something wrong with my money?'

"'No,' said Yigdol, 'and there's nothing wrong with my brain, though my eyes are failing, but even failing, they see too much and ask too many questions, which may be why the Almighty is taking them back. They ask, where did this young man come from, why is he frightened, why does he buy two suits, and why does he keep so much money in his side pocket and pretend to be so little?'

"'I'm a tailor,' explained Yigdol. 'I notice bulges, tears, and faces. Don't fold your bills and don't keep them in your pants pocket. That is what peasants do. One might wonder why a peasant has so much money. These clothes may make you look like a shopkeeper, but you must act to fit the clothes.'

"'What do you want of me?' I said with my eyes on the man at the same time I sought a weapon in the corners or on the table. The scissors and knife were within reach. 'I'll pay no more than we agreed on.'

"Yigdol laughed. 'I want the promised land,' he said. 'I want it now. Can you pay me that? I want no more of your money than we agreed upon. You have nothing to fear from me.'

"'You think I'm funny,' I said in some confusion.

"Yigdol shook his head no and pushed the glasses up on his ample nose.

"'No, I think you are afraid and could use some help. You are running from the Revolution. You are from the south. You have the accent. You are heading north, for Riga, the sea?'

"'Yes, for Riga.'

"Yigdol smiled proudly at the confirmation of his deduction. "'Go to Palestine,' he said.

"'Perhaps,' I said. 'Yes, perhaps.' I said it as if I were really considering it, but I was not. Yigdol, with his failing eyes, saw through me and gave an amused look that shook my confidence.

"'I have a carriage to sell,' I said.

"'A carriage? A good carriage such as a well-to-do shopkeeper might have?'

"'Yes,' I said, clutching the two suits to my chest.

"'If you drive your fine carriage down this street as far as the street goes, you will find a market. In the market you will see a wagon. The wagon has no wheels. It is a store from which a fat man sells geese. Say to that fat man that Yigdol suggested you see him about your fine carriage. But you would do well to put on your new suit before you do so.'

"I reached in my pocket for more money.

"'No more money,' said Yigdol, raising his hand, a needle pressed tightly between thumb and finger, a filament of thread swaying against the dusty light. 'I don't know what you are or what you are doing. I am simply a man helping another man.'

"Yigdol smiled, and I tried to smile back, but I had no idea of why we were smiling. I escaped quickly through the door and hurried through the town with my bundle in hand, circling the puddles the children played in.

"I found Abraham talking to the horse and threw him his new clothes. Twenty minutes later we drove into Gomel in our fine carriage and new clothes, with Abraham smiling proudly and me feeling like a fool in disguise. The market was easy to find in an uncrowded, open, uncobbled area with a ring of carts and crates, squawking chickens and geese, and a few goats. The people in the market, sellers and buyers, all stopped to watch the two well-dressed young men in the carriage. I considered telling Abraham to drive straight through quickly, but he held back and played his part. The fat man near the broken wagon sat like a rock, watching me as I got down and moved toward him. An old woman and a young girl stood next to him, the girl no more than eight or nine, keeping her hand in the old woman's as if I or someone else might steal her.

"'Yigdol the tailor said you might be interested in buying a carriage?'"

"'I am interested in buying what I can sell,' said the fat man in an incredibly high voice that belied his body as he pulled his jacket tight around him. 'I'm interested in staying alive. I'm interested in keeping my mother here and my son's daughter alive.'

"'What can you give me for the carriage?'

"'I can give you a little money for the carriage and the horse and a little advice. The advice will be worth more than the money. The carriage is not yours, and you'd best get rid of it quickly before you are asked questions you can't answer. That's a good horse, but it will have to be slaughtered for its meat. A chance can't be taken that it will be recognized. This is the money I'll give with that advice, and I'll tell you how to get on a train that will take you to . . .' He waited.

"'Riga,' I said.

"'Of course, Riga. I'll have someone take you to the train in Minsk and buy your tickets for a slight price. The ticket man is a half Jew. He'll put you in a car where no one will ask you questions until you get to Riga. For this you will pay me. Subtracted from what I will pay you for the horse and carriage, which can be my death, you owe me thirty rubles.'

"'The Jews of Gomel are very clever,' I said.

"'The Jews of Gomel have to be very clever or there would soon be no Jews of Gomel. Isn't it that way in your village?'

"'It is.'

"'We have a bargain?'

"'Yes,' I said, and paid the man. The little girl looked at me and backed away.

"'Her father, my son, left her last year and went to America,' explained the fat man, counting the money I gave him and nodding to a thin young man, who moved forward to take the horse and carriage from Abraham. I nodded to Abraham to let the young man take them, and he reluctantly got down and watched the horse and cart being led into a large barnlike door in a stone building behind the broken wagon.

"'He's going to send for her?' I said.

"The fat man shrugged.

"The thin young man came back with an older, heavier

horse and a wagon, not a carriage. The fat man made a pushing move with his hand to indicate that we should climb in the wagon. We did, and the fat man immediately turned to his business of negotiating with a sagging woman over the price of a goose.

"There was straw in the wagon and a few blankets. We gave the driver some money to buy food for the trip, and I lay back with his sack for a pillow and tried to sleep, my head rolling against the brass candlestick.

"We spent two days in the wagon, getting out only to relieve ourselves, sitting up only to eat the food brought by the young driver, who said nothing, did not even give his name.

"Minsk began almost an hour before we reached the train station, first with farms and then a few inns and small factories, followed by a few blacksmiths and clusters of homes and shops. When we reached the cobbled streets, buildings began to rise on both sides, some four stories tall. A platoon of firemen lounged in front of a fire station, their uniforms military and their hats shined metal.

"From the wagon we could see that most of the men we passed were unshaven and not Jewish. There were carriages going past with finely dressed women with wide hats, and then we passed a synagogue, the largest I had ever seen.

"Without thinking, I moved closer to the young driver, resenting him but dependent. At the train station, the young man went in and purchased the tickets while we got down from the wagon and stretched our legs.

"'There is a train for Riga in five hours. Sit on a bench and pretend you are sleeping till the train comes. Then get on the train and go to the third class, next to the last car. Eat the food you have with you and stay away from the front of the train and the Russians.'

"It was all the young man said to us, and he was gone without looking back. We found a space on a bench next to a tree stump of a father and fat son in clean work clothes. The father and son ate garlic sausage and talked. For five hours we pretended to sleep. The train was another hour late, and we pretended to sleep some more. I needed a toilet but was afraid to leave the bench.

"The platform was filled with passengers, many of them Russian soldiers, one of whom bumped into me when a few of them playfully pushed each other. The man fell momentarily in my lap, but I pretended to sleep through the incident. I didn't even know which side of the Revolution the soldiers were on.

"When the train arrived, we got to the next to last car. People were sitting on all the benches, but we found space on the floor near the window wall. There were pockets of conversations, including a low conversation about something called Zionism held between two shabbily dressed men. When I could stand it no longer, I asked someone where the toilet was. To get to it, I would have to move to the front of the train through the Russian soldiers. Instead, I made my way to the space between the two cars and urinated into the night.

"In two days and many stops the word 'Riga' spread through the car. People began to check their cloth sacks and thin suitcases, to prepare, though the word was we were still many hours away. Abraham smiled, and I nodded, touching the flattened roll of bills in my jacket.

"When the train jerked into Riga, the people spewed forth as if they were already in America or England. We tried to stay in the middle of the crowd. The Russian soldiers got off, joking about the smell of the people still pushing each other and the crowd.

"A trio of soldiers and officers forced their way through the confusion and headed right past us. To clear the way, the officers pushed with their sticks and hands, moving against the flow of the crowd. One young officer stood in front of me and prodded me with his stick.

"The soldier was amused at what looked like a confrontation with a simpleminded Jew, and he turned to his comrades to share the joke. They looked equally amused.

"We followed the crowd into the darkness to a vast foggy waterfront where thousands of people sat on their luggage, talking, looking at the huge metal boat with peeling paint, a boat that was as big as the entire village of Yekteraslav, maybe as big as two Yekteraslavs.

"I grabbed the arm of a well-dressed Jewish woman who was talking to another well-dressed woman seated on a trio of matching cloth suitcases. The woman turned on me in anger, but something in my face frightened her, and she stood mute.

" 'Tell me,' I whispered, my voice cracking. 'How do we get on that boat. Where is it going?'

" 'To America,' the woman said. She was about thirty, not pretty but womanly.

" 'You have to get an exit visa,' the woman said. 'You go to the end of the dock. If you didn't get one in your district, you go there and stand in line.'

" 'And,' said her friend, an overflowing older woman with a very wide hat, 'when you get in, you tell them you want to go and you pay them a bribe, and they make you wait a few days. If you don't bribe, you wait a week or two weeks or ten, but you go, anyway. You go because you are Jewish, and they want to get rid of you as much as you want to go.'

" 'I know,' I said.

" 'Yes,' said the woman, whose arm I still held. I let her loose, and Abraham and I walked in the direction to the visa shack, stepping over sleeping families, couples huddled together. The heavy mist from the sea and the ship drifted over the crowd, a cloud that covered clumps of people, that blanketed but didn't protect us.

"Shifting my sack from one shoulder to the next a dozen times, I finally found a long line stretching for what looked like miles. We watched the line for fifteen minutes, but it did not move.

" 'The office is closed until the morning,' said a man we were standing in front of. Abraham and I had made the man nervous, and the fellow, a frayed creature in a gray foreign-looking suit, wanted us to be gone. 'Go to the end and wait till it opens.'

"We nodded and moved toward the end, a hike almost as long as the one we had taken from the two women to the line itself. We sat at the rear behind two old couples and watched an old man with a long beard hugging himself hard to keep out the cold, though the night was not as terrible as others we had suffered in the last two weeks. I watched Abraham's eyes turning into the night mist in the direction of Yekteraslav, not expecting to see anything but unable to turn away.

"'You want a visa?'

"The voice was soft, pleading; the words in Yiddish I found hard to understand. I turned my eyes to the voice and automatically put my hand out to protect my jacket and money. The man before me was short, almost a dwarf. He was clean-shaven, and his mouth showed an incredibly jagged line of teeth, distorting his face so that he had a permanent look, which might have been a smile or a grimace of pain.

"'You want a visa?' repeated the little man.

"'Yes,' I said. 'We need visas.'

"'And a passage on that ship?' the little man said, nodding back toward the dock.

"'Yes,' I said.

"'Can you pay?' said the man.

"The old man, hugging himself, leaned into the conversation and looked at the little man.

"'He's a *shtupper*,' said the old man. 'A pig sticker. He gets people who don't want to leave to sell him visas, and then he resells them, taking places away from people who should be on the ships.'

"'You don't know,' hissed the little man. 'You old cocker. You don't know.'

"'How much do you want?' I said, grabbing at the possibility of immediately departing from fear and memory.

"'Maybe more than you can pay?'

"I reached out and grabbed the little man by the collar, clapping my hand over his mouth to quiet him. The feel of the wet mouth disgusted me.

"'Just tell me.'

"'Show me what you have,' whispered the little man.

"I turned my back and pulled out my money, but the man had maneuvered to see it.

"'I'll take that,' said the little man. 'All of it.'

"'Show me the visas and the tickets,' I demanded.

"The little man pulled a crumpled package from his pocket and held it out. Inside the package was a folded piece of cardboard.

"'That's only one visa, one ticket,' I said, looking at Abraham, who had said nothing, only looked like a frightened cow since we had descended into the nightmare of Riga.

"The old man nodded yes, that he had only one ticket, one visa, that we would have to make up our minds if we wanted it. I said no, and lifted my sack, stepping out of line and back into the mist and the tangle of waiting bodies. Abraham hesitated and followed. He said something to the old man, who nodded, and I called over my shoulder to Abraham to join with me. I'll tell you the truth. I planned to find two people, get them out of line behind a shack and take their tickets and, if need be, their lives, but I never got the chance. Abraham and I huddled in the chill fog behind a storage shack on the dock, and I dozed. Being hit is supposed to knock you out. It woke me for an instant like a headache, and I found myself looking up at Abraham, who stood over me, my mother's candlestick in his hand. He brought the candlestick down again on my head. I was stunned, couldn't move, blood coming into my eyes. I'm sure he took me for dead. I know I was unconscious.

"When I woke up, it was just dawn. My sack was gone. The money was gone. I lurched to the dock as people were boarding the ship, and I could see Abraham in the crowd. He saw me, too, and fear was in his eyes. I tried to get on the ship, tried to push past the people crowding the gangplank, screamed like a mad bloody fool, and was thrown from the dock by ship's guards.

"I had passed out again and lay there, in the crowd gathering for the next ship. People moved around me, waiting for me to die. Some went through my pockets. I could feel it, but there was nothing to take. Abraham, my friend from childhood, had taken everything. Obviously, I did not die. I was too stubborn to die. I crawled away that night, stole some food, and the next day, when I felt strong enough, I washed my face in stinging seawater and found a solitary man who had a ticket and a visa. His name was Vasili Rosnechikov. I became Vasili Rosnechikov, and I got on the next ship with a small sack of food purchased with Vasili Rosnechikov's money. Two hours later I felt the boat creak and lurch and heard sailors running around and yelling, heard old women crying and being comforted by old men, heard young people laugh with joy, touched with fear of the unknown future, but I sat looking at my filthy hands and the deck of the ship, not back at the shore, at Russia. I was on my way to America to kill Abraham Savitskaya."

The story had taken a half hour or more, but Rostnikov had not interrupted it. It had been an old man's story, a story remembered or imagined in vivid detail, the fairy tale of his life, the justification for his existence. In the corner near the door to the restaurant, Zelach had begun to slouch, losing whatever alertness he had managed to muster. Tkach, mindful of recent embarrassment, stood alert. Martin, the gunman, had folded his arms and leaned back, refusing drinks from the bottle shared by the policeman and Posniky.

"And so," said Rostnikov, pouring himself and Posniky the last of the bottle and feeling slightly drunk, "you went to America and were unable to find Savitskaya."

"I did not find him," Posniky agreed, clenching his worn teeth and remembering his frustration. "I found other things while I looked. I found how to take care of myself. I—let us just say that I made a good living. I raised a family. I have grandchildren, even two great-grandchildren. I don't show photographs anymore. I can't remember which one has which name. But I kept looking for Abraham. I almost caught up to him in St. Louis."

"That is in Missouri," said Rostnikov with pride.

"Right," agreed Posniky. "But he found out I was after him. Then I found he had come back to Russia. He came back here to hide from me, came back with my mother's candlestick. Through contacts I found that he had a protector who had helped him get back into Russia, to get away from me; at least that's what they said."

"And who was this protector?" asked Rostnikov, knowing that he would have to rise soon or his leg would lock in pain.

The old man shrugged. "Whoever it was"—he sighed—"he didn't protect him this time. You can't imagine the feeling I've lived with, the feeling of unfinished business. You wake up with it every morning."

"Like finding the last few pages missing from a mystery novel you like and knowing the book is so old that you will probably never know the ending," said Rostnikov.

"Exactly," said the old man, looking up and brushing back his mane of colorless hair.

"And now?"

"And now," said Posniky with resignation, "I am finished. I've read you the last two pages of your mystery, and you can close the book. A question: is there some way we can get Martin on the plane? Somehow this reminds me of that day in Riga sixty years ago. Only this time it is me and Martin and an airplane."

Martin, hearing his name mentioned, came alert and looked at the two men.

"We will see," said Rostnikov, starting to get up. "But not now. I think we must now go to my office for an official statement." Posniky leaned forward, and for an instant Porfiry Petrovich feared that the tough old man was going to have a heart attack or cry. Instead, he reached under the table and came up with a brown package, which clearly contained the brass candlestick.

"Let's go," he said, but Martin was not prepared to go without trouble. He pushed his chair back, looked to the two doors, chose Tkach's, and ran toward him. Rostnikov reached out to grab him but was too late. Martin bumped into one table where a couple was eating soup, which went flying.

Rostnikov could but watch as Martin, a head taller and

much more solid, rushed at Tkach, who appeared to step to the side to let him pass. When Martin hit the hinged kitchen door, he threw Tkach a quick warning look that Tkach answered with a solid right fist to Martin's throat. Martin twisted, clutching his throat, and Tkach hit him again with a nearby chair.

Customers watched. Women screamed, and Zelach ambled over to help subdue the writhing American.

"He's still young," said Posniky, who was standing at Rostnikov's side with the candlestick under his arm. "He doesn't know when he has lost. I was the same. Let's go, chief inspector."

Ignoring the crowd, which seemed to realize that a police or KGB action was taking place, Zelach and Tkach handcuffed Martin's hands behind him and led him out behind Rostnikov and Posniky, who moved slowly through the lobby and onto the sidewalk.

"This is the first time I have been in Moscow," Posniky said, looking around. "When I was a boy, my family wouldn't let us come to the city. They thought Jews were routinely slaughtered on the streets of Moscow."

Rostnikov turned to watch Zelach shove the gasping, angry Martin forward. The turn, as it was, probably saved Rostnikov's life. A dark car screeched down the street away from the curb. It roared in front of a taxi that was just pulling away from the Metropole, leaped the curb, and hit Posniky, who had no idea that it was coming. The fender of the moving car missed Rostnikov by a shadow as he fell back to the sidewalk. Posniky was sucked under the car and disappeared for an instant, though Rostnikov could hear his body thud against the undercarriage of the automobile. Then the car jerked forward, hitting a young woman, who was lifted into the air. From the rear of the black car Posniky's twisted, bloody body was spat out toward the seated Rostnikov. The packaged brass candlestick was still clutched tightly in the gnarled hand of the corpse.

NINE

AS THE CAR HAD STRUCK POSNIKY, A THOUGHT HAD struck Rostnikov. The driver's face had been covered with a scarf even in the hot evening, but Rostnikov was sure of two things about that driver. First, that it was a man and not a woman. Second, that it was not an old man. He was also certain, even as the car deposited the body before him, that it had been no accident. The eyes of the driver had not been shrouded by drink. They had been quite cold, quite firm, quite professional.

There was a silent fraction of a second when the world stopped and everyone and everything froze, everything but the dark car speeding away down the avenue. Rostnikov knew from experience that the silent moment was so slight, so nearly imperceptible, that only those who had learned to experience it even noticed it existed. He had never discussed that halting of time with anyone, had savored it secretly, wondered at how many thoughts, ideas, insights, came during that hush. And then it was over.

Women were screaming. The handcuffed American lurched forward and tripped, sprawling hard on his face and smashing his nose. Tkach leaned over to pick him up as Zelach shambled over to the woman who had been hit by the car that had ground the old man to rags. People rushed out of the hotel. One man actually ran down the street after the disappearing automobile. The world, following the silent moment, rushed by, and Rostnikov felt himself moving slowly, letting madness wave past him. He knelt and removed the candlestick from the old man's dead hand.

"Call an ambulance," shouted Zelach from the stricken woman whom he was tending. "You," he said, pointing to one of the hotel clerks who had rushed out. "Call now."

Martin was on his knees, his nose crushed, eyes wide open, and Tkach was using his own handkerchief to stop the bleeding.

"I must go, Sasha," Rostnikov said, tucking the candlestick under his right arm.

Tkach looked up from his prisoner with a question but held it back when he saw Rostnikov's face. The Washtub was somewhere else. For a moment Tkach thought that the chief inspector might be in shock from the hit-and-run, the crushed body, the near miss, but he was sure that what he saw in that worn face was a disturbing thought.

"Where can I reach you?" Tkach said. Already down the street a police car was screeching through the night.

"I'm not sure. I may be at the home of Lev Ostrovsky or at the Moscow Art Theatre, the old one. Old men are dying."

That old men were dying seemed perfectly normal to Tkach, who was a young man, but he looked at the pieces of bone and flesh that had once been Mikhail Posniky, and he nodded.

Five uniformed policemen appeared from nowhere and began to hold the crowd back. Rostnikov and the candlestick moved past the policemen and into the small crowd. He broke through and found himself moving through a traffic jam.

"What happened?" a fat woman in a gray dress asked him.

"An old man died," he said absently, and walked on.

He had Lev Ostrovsky's address in his pocket, but he was closer to the theater and decided to head there first. He was probably too late, but he had to try. Of course, he might be wrong. There were many possibilities. The black car could already have visited Lev Ostrovsky. Or it might now be on its way to find him. Or someone else might be taking care of Ostrovsky. Or Porfiry Petrovich Rostnikov might be entirely wrong.

The taxi driver looked at him suspiciously, eyed the heavy package under the arm of the square man with the bad leg, and wondered whether it was a gun or a bar to hit him with and take his money. The driver, whose name was Ivan Ivanov, was very sensitive to the commonness of his name, the anonymity of his existence. There were times when he wondered if anyone would miss one more or less Ivan Ivanov.

"Where?" he said, shifting his roll of rubles from his pocket to the space under the seat cushion.

"Moscow Art Theatre," Rostnikov said. "I'm a policeman. Hurry."

Ivan Ivanov looked up in his mirror, examined the face of the man, decided that he was a policeman, and hoped that the five bottles of vodka he had under the seat would not rattle as he drove. He did hurry to the theater, not so much because he wanted to please the dour policeman but to get rid of him.

Rostnikov removed his tie when he got out of the cab and paid the fare. He shoved his change into his trouser pocket along with the tie and headed for the same door through which he had gone before.

This time a pair of men sat at a table just inside the door. One man, lean and gray, wore a cap on his head. The other man, younger, fine featured, sat against the table, his arms folded.

"Police," Rostnikov said, holding up his identification card.

The gray man shrugged.

"They're that way, stage. Remind them there's a performance tonight and we have to set up," he said, turning back to the younger man, who looked as if he had been interrupted in the middle of a story he wanted to get back to.

"Who's that way?" said Rostnikov.

"The other policemen."

"Maybe it's a police festival, a cultural evening," said

the younger man, looking away from Rostnikov.

"How many of them?" Rostnikov asked. "How many policemen?"

"Two," said the gray man, rubbing his stubby chin.

Rostnikov hurried down the narrow hallway, following the turns, remembering the way. Behind him he could hear the sound of the younger man's voice saying something sarcastic, but he couldn't make it out. When he made the first turn, Rostnikov ripped the brown paper from the candlestick and threw it in a corner. He hurried as quickly as his leg would allow him to the small door that led to the stage. He held the heavy candlestick up, imagining Posniky using it before Rostnikov was even born to smash the skulls of his victims on the road, imagining Abraham Savitskaya bringing the brass weight down on Posniky on the dock at Riga.

He opened the door as quietly as he could and heard nothing, just the creaks of an old theater. He worked his way up the stairs, which ached beneath him and whimpered his presence like the lyre of Bulba, which gave away the presence of the holy thief in the fairy tale. He held the magic candlestick and followed the dim light, avoiding rope, chairs, and lights as he moved, listening to his own breathing, hearing no voices.

There were a dozen lights on the stage, and the audience area was once again dark. The stage was set. It looked like a garden, a summer-house garden with artificial acacia trees and lilacs covering most of a small house with two windows and a little glass-enclosed porch.

Rostnikov moved slowly onto the stage and put his foot on the steps leading up to the porch. Then he heard something stir inside the door in front of him. He took the next step, held the candlestick above his head in his right hand, and opened the door with his left.

He came very close to bringing the candlestick down on the head of Lev Ostrovsky, who stumbled forward into his arms with a groan. He was bird light, and Rostnikov didn't even step back from the impact. Rostnikov looked around quickly and knelt to place the old man against the steps.

"Who did this?" Rostnikov whispered, for what had been done was quite evident to Rostnikov simply by looking at the bleached white old face. He had been beaten by someone who had been careful not to touch his face. The thin body was broken around the rib cage. A busy medical examiner would probably think the ancient man had simply stumbled and fallen.

"'I know,'" he smiled, using his ebbing strength to put his finger to his nose. "'I'm a cunning fellow. Life gets to be very difficult unless you dissemble. I often play the fool and the innocent who doesn't know what he's doing. That helps a lot in keeping all that's trivial and vulgar at arm's length.'"

"What are you—?"

Ostrovsky looked around, wisps of hair dangling down his forehead. "We're doing *Queer People* tonight. Gorky. My favorite. I'm doing Mastakov's final lines. They suit me."

"Ostrovsky," Rostnikov asked again, cradling the old man's head in his lap. "Who did this?" But the old eyes turned toward the dark seats, and his voice quivered into lines remembered.

"'Sometimes I appear ludicrous, in spite of myself. I know that. But knowing it, when I notice I'm being ludicrous, I turn this to my advantage, too, as a means of self-defense. You think it's wrong? Perhaps it is. But it saves one from trivial worries.'"

He paused, looked at Rostnikov for a moment, and went on. "'Life is more interesting and more honest than human beings.'"

"Are you still Mastakov?" Rostnikov said gently.

"You couldn't tell?" asked Ostrovsky in a fading voice, a tiny smile on his lips.

"I-couldn't tell," said Rostnikov.

"Shmuel Prensky," the old man said, closing his eyes and licking his dry lips. "Shmuel sent them to kill me. I knew it would happen, but I got to play a death scene."

"Yes," said Rostnikov. "You played it beautifully."

"One more line," said Ostrovsky, his voice almost gone,

his eyes still closed. "Mastakov's final line. 'Don't forgive what I did, but forget it—will you?' "

Rostnikov sat, silently feeling the man's breath grow shallow. The old eyes fluttered, and the detective had to lean forward, his ear almost touching the dry mouth to hear.

"You get the final line," the old man said. "Elena's line."

"What is the line?"

" 'I will,' " came Ostrovsky's final breath.

"I will not forget," said Rostnikov to the dead man, placing his head gently on the steps.

In the rear of the dark theater a door opened. A square of light showed two figures who had apparently been listening from the rear of the theater. One of the shadows turned for an instant and faced Rostnikov. It may have been a trick of the distance or the light or his state of mind, but Rostnikov thought the hands of the figure came together in a slow mockery of applause. Then the door closed, and Rostnikov was alone.

Anna Timofeyeva lived not far from the Moscow River in a one-room apartment with her cat Baku. As a deputy procurator, she could have had a larger apartment, a better address, more privacy. The only concession she had made to her status was to request her own toilet and bath. She had used her power for this convenience.

Since her third heart attack, she had received conflicting medical advice on what she should do. Two doctors told her to rest, relax, do as little as possible, lull the damaged heart into dreamy function, not demand too much of it, not make it angry. Treat it, in short, like a delicate bomb implanted in her chest. She preferred the advice of the doctor Porfiry Petrovich had sent, a sullen Jew named Alex who had looked at her dumpy body, examined her stock of food, and told her to get out and walk more each day. First a mile. Next two miles. Eventually four miles. She would not have to do what so many Muscovites were doing—buying American-style jogging suits made in Italy and dashing around the streets almost before the sun came up.

And so she had taken to walking, to seeing Moscow, which she had really never done till now. She would walk, eat carefully, as Doctor Alex had prescribed, and have long talks with Baku. She read, watched a bit of television, and adjusted reasonably well to her idleness after a lifetime of eighteen-hour-a-day dedication to her work, a dedication that had exhausted her body. She didn't regret her life. On the contrary, she had treated herself like a machine, knowing that the machine could not last forever, would have to be replaced by another machine. She was, however, not particularly pleased by Khabolov, the nonmachine that had replaced her, but that was not her responsibility.

At first, Anna Timofeyeva had worn her uniform on the few occasions when she had reason to go out in public since her last attack. The people in her apartment building who knew her slightly continued to call her comrade procurator, but it soon seemed an act to her, and she had given up the uniform, content instead to wear slacks and loose-fitting men's shirts. She owned a few dresses but never wore them. Even hanging in the closet, they looked like the clothes of a laundry sack. The thought amused her. Rostnikov was a washtub and she a laundry sack. They had worked well together.

She was sitting at her small table near the window, sharing a dinner of potato broth, bread, and sliced tomatoes with Baku, who purred, closed his eyes, and paused to rub his heavy orange body against her. Then came the knock and she said, "Come in, Porfiry Petrovich," and in he came.

"You know my knock?" he said, stepping in. Baku looked up suspiciously, recognized him, and went back to his broth.

"That, and I was thinking about you. You want some soup?"

Rostnikov shrugged and placed the candlestick on the table as she got up, pulled a bowl from the nearby small cupboard, and poured him a bowl of soup from the pot on the small burner.

She didn't ask him if he wanted bread, simply gave him a dark slice.

"A present?" she said, looking at the candlestick.

"You wouldn't want it," he said. "If I were religious, I would say it is haunted. Perhaps it must be returned to its rightful owner, but I think that owner is dead." He dipped a piece of bread into the soup, sopped up the liquid, and then ate it. The soup was unseasoned, though hot. Anna Timofeyeva was not a good cook.

"That's what you have come to tell me? A fairy tale about a brass candlestick?"

"No," he said. "I've come to ask your advice, perhaps for your help. Three old men are dead. It is somewhat complicated, but two of them were killed by another old man named Shmuel Prensky, a fourth man."

He paused, but the name of Prensky meant nothing to her.

"Your successor has told me not to pursue this case, that I have been denied access to central files." He finished his bread by placing a slice of tomato on it and downing the half sandwich in two bites.

"And . . ." she said while he swallowed his food.

"And I want to get into the files. I want to find Shmuel Prensky."

He told her the entire story, from the moment he was assigned the case through his finding of the body of Lev Ostrovsky. A look he recognized had come over her. He imagined her back in her office, uniform tight, the picture of Lenin in his monastic room over her head as she weighed possibilities.

"If you go back to Petrovka, you will have to drop the case. Khabolov will dismiss you."

Rostnikov agreed and reached over to pet Baku, who lay on the table watching him.

"You have dropped the Savitskaya case," she said. "You can call in and so report. The killer confessed and was run down by a hit-and-run driver. The case is closed. I still have a phone. You can do it from here."

"And then?" he said.

"Then you pursue the case of the murdered old actor. It is a different case. He gave you the name of Shmuel Prensky."

"I need the files," Rostnikov said, sighing.

"And you want me to get them for you," she said, standing up to remove the dishes. "I have taken to drinking one glass of wine each night. Your doctor, Alex, prescribed it. You'll have a glass?"

She brought two glasses and a dark bottle from the cupboard.

"It's Greek wine," she said. "A gift from the chief procurator, who has, I'm sure, dismissed me from his mind, which is understandable. He has not, however, revoked my privileges, as you well know."

"So," he said, taking the wine she poured for him in a ktichen glass.

"So, I will do it. We will get a taxi after you call in, and I will go to the central files. If the name of Shmuel Prensky is there, I will find it. I warn you, I am very poor with those computers. If the information is new, I probably will have difficulty with it."

"This is an old man, comrade Anna, a very old man. His deeds are buried in Soviet antiquity."

She shrugged and smiled, happy to be active.

"Make your call and watch the television. I may be an hour or more."

Before she left, he called Petrovka and left a message for the assistant procurator, indicating that the killer of Abraham Savitskaya had almost accidentally fallen into his lap and that the case was now ended and he was going out for dinner and a movie. The operator at Petrovka indicated that Procurator Khabolov was trying to reach him, but Rostnikov sighed and said he would come to see the assistant procurator first thing in the morning.

After Anna Timofeyeva left, he stroked Baku, who leaped heavily onto his lap, sipped Greek wine, and watched a travel show on the television. The show was about Hong Kong and made the Oriental city look like a vast, noisy illuminated toy. He wanted to visit Hong Kong now almost as much as he wanted to see America.

After an hour he called home and told Sarah he was working late. She told him Josef had called and would be in for a short visit in a few days. She sounded genuinely happy, and Rostnikov sensed that things were going better for him at home. Sarah also said that calls had come every half hour for Rostnikov to get in touch with Procurator Khabolov.

"I have called in," he said. "I will see Comrade Khabolov in the morning. Meanwhile, I must eat, perhaps take in a show, and pursue another case for at least a few hours."

Sarah said, "I understand," and by the way she said it, he was sure that she did, indeed, understand. Their phone had been tapped since his unsuccessful attempt to blackmail the KGB into letting him emigrate to the United States. While the tap was often an inconvenience, it could sometimes be used to bolster his lies and deceptions. He hung up the phone to wait.

Anna Timofeyeva came back almost three hours after she had left and found Rostnikov dozing in a straight-backed chair with Baku asleep on his lap. She sat down in front of him and shook his right leg.

"I'm awake," he said without opening his eyes. "You had trouble?"

"I had trouble," she said, and his eyes opened. "The traces of Shmuel Prensky are very old, comrade, very old. References to him exist going back to 1932. He held minor positions in the Stalin rise, and then he disappeared. He was a Jew. Many Jews disappeared. You know that."

"But now he has appeared again." Rostnikov sighed, placing Baku gently on the chair he vacated.

"I'll do more tomorrow," she said. "The records are old. The strings are thin. The boxes heavy. The clerks irritable."

"Thank you, Anna Timofeyeva," he said, going to the door.

"We'll talk tomorrow, Porfiry Petrovich," she said. "It felt good to be active. I'll walk an extra mile tomorrow."

He waved his candlestick to her and the cat and left.

Rostnikov's initial plan was to walk home. It was about four miles, but the sky was now clear and the evening cool. He walked, candlestick under his arm, unaware of the people who moved out of his path, deep in thought. He had gone no more than a mile when he knew his leg would permit no further exercise. Besides, he longed for, needed, his weights, needed the strain of muscle to clear the wine and confusion. As he turned his head, looking for the light of the metro station he had just passed, a cab pulled up to the curb.

Through the open window, the cab driver, wearing a black cap, called, "You want a cab?"

Rostnikov opened the door, got in wearily, sat back with his candlestick, and closed his eyes. The cab eased into the night traffic and jostled him comfortably. Less than ten minutes later, the cab pulled up in front of Rostnikov's apartment building. Instead of paying, Rostnikov sat silently waiting, looking at the back of the cab driver's head. Rostnikov had not given the driver a destination, had not given his address. He had waited for the man to ask, but when the question had not come, he had sat back to absorb and wait, the candlestick ready in his hand.

"Tomorrow morning at six, no later," the driver said. "You are to report to KGB headquarters. You are not to leave your apartment tonight. Colonel Drozhkin will be expecting you."

Rostnikov got out of the cab without offering to pay and made his way wearily through the door and up the stairs.

TEN

IN THE MORNING, SARAH ROSTNIKOV ROLLED OVER IN bed and examined the face of her husband. His eyes were open and appeared to be examining the ceiling with great interest. His behavior the night before had been most strange. She had been too much within herself, too much concerned with disappointment to worry about Porfiry Petrovich, and since he seemed content in his routine, she had not thought greatly about his problems, though she knew they were great and many.

When he had come home late the night before, he had eaten without noticing what he ate, had lifted his weights, losing himself so completely that she had to remind him that it was well past midnight and the clanking of the metal on the mat in the corner was surely disturbing the neighbors. Misha and Alexiana Korkov would never complain. They were a mousy pair with a pale, near-teen daughter. Misha sold tickets at the USSR Economic Achievements Exhibition, while Alexiana did something vague and menial at the Aeroflot Air Terminal.

After he had stopped lifting, Rostnikov had sat on his small bench, sweating, thinking, distant. He had washed, and for the first time in memory, at least her memory, he had not read at least a few pages of an American detective novel. It had become a ritual need of her husband's to read at least a few pages of Ed McBain or Lawrence Block, Bill Pronzini, or Joseph Wambaugh. He was forever ferreting out their novels in English, hoarding them, fearing that he would run out. But last night he read nothing.

Stranger still, he had asked her if she wanted to make love. He had said it so softly, almost an exhaled breath with words, that she almost missed it. Sarah had been tired, concerned, hot, and far from any feeling of passion, but there was something in her husband that made the request a near plea. It was a sound she had never heard from him before. No one else would have noticed it. The man was so solid, so confident, so unmovable, that his possible vulnerability frightened her.

And now, in the morning, the sun coming through the window's thin curtains, she said, "Porfiry, what is it?"

"I must get up," he said. "I have an appointment."

He sat up, scratched his broad, hard, and hairy belly through his white undershirt, and reached over to massage his leg. At least this part of the ritual did not change.

"Where are you going?" she tried.

Rostnikov looked at his wife, her long, red-tinged hair back over her shoulders, framing her round, still-handsome face.

"Porfiry?"

"It's better you do not know," he said, getting up and reaching for his pants. Sarah had sewn the sleeve the evening before, and it looked fine. He had but two suits and liked to keep the other one for emergencies and when his regular suit was being cleaned. Getting it cleaned was a major chore. So much was a major chore, he thought, looking for his shirt.

"You'll call me later?" she said. "I'll be home by six. Is this dangerous?"

Rostnikov had one shirt-sleeve on. He paused, pondering the question. "I don't know," he said.

"Are you—are you afraid?" she asked, a question she never imagined asking him. She could tell by his broad, flat face that he had not considered this. Before he answered, he finished putting on his shirt.

"I don't think so," he said, buttoning his shirt and searching for his tie. "I am curious, filled with curiosity. If you ask me, is this dangerous, Porfiry? I say, yes. I think so. But it is a puzzle, a page that must be turned even if the page is on fire and I burn my hand."

She was still in bed, watching him, when he finished dressing. He moved to her, kissed both her cheeks and her forehead.

"If Josef gets here before I do, do not eat without me," he said. "If I am not back by nine, call Tkach at Petrovka."

"Porfiry," she said, feeling fear.

He shook his head no and pursed his lips. Then he turned and went out the door. Sarah tried to hold that memory of him, to etch it in her mind. She didn't want to tell herself why she was doing this, but she knew, she knew deep within her, that she feared never seeing him again.

Rostnikov was more familiar with the huge yellow-gray building at 22 Lubyanka Street than he really wanted to be. He walked up the small rise toward the building, past the thirty-six-foot statue of "Iron" Felix Dzerzhinsky, who organized the Cheka for Lenin. The Cheka, after many transformations, was now the KGB.

The building, like the others that flanked it and were part of the KGB complex, was unmarked. Before the Revolution, the building had belonged to the All-Russian Insurance Company. Captured German soldiers and political prisoners built a nine-story annex after World War II. The old section circles a courtyard. On one side of the courtyard is Lubyanka Prison where thousands have been led to execution cells.

Rostnikov walked slowly up the steps of the main building at 2 Dzerzhinsky Square. He passed a pair of men coming out, both of whom had the somber look of agents. They did not look at him.

And then Rostnikov was through the door and standing in the complex known as the Center. Another KGB building existed on the Outer Ring Road where foreign operations were handled. Rostnikov had passed it, at least the place where he knew it existed. It could not be viewed from the road. Meanwhile, the Center continued as the heart of the KGB operation.

Rostnikov moved through the outer lobby, absorbing the building again. The walls and hallways were, he knew, all a uniform light green, and the parquet floors, except those of the generals, a few colonels, and the division leaders, were uncarpeted. Throughout the complex, lighting came from large, round ceiling globes covered with shades.

"Porfiry Petrovich Rostnikov," he told the uniformed young man at the desk. Behind this uniformed man stood another young man, in uniform, carrying a small automatic weapon and standing at full attention.

"Chief Inspector Rostnikov," Rostnikov added.

"Wait there," the young officer said, pointing to a series of nearby wooden chairs. Rostnikov sat. He sat for about fifteen minutes, watching people come in and out, noting that everyone seemed to whisper as if they were in a cathedral or Lenin's tomb.

Then an older officer in uniform appeared before Rostnikov, ramrod straight, and said, "Come."

And Rostnikov came. As had happened the other times he had been there, his guide moved at march pace, easily outdistancing the policeman, who simply tried to keep his guide in sight until the man realized the distance and slowed down. But in this case Rostnikov knew where they were headed, knew the door they stopped in front of, recognized the gravelly voice that answered the guide's knock. There was no name on the door, no marking.

"Come," said the voice, and Rostnikov entered alone and closed the door behind him—dark brown carpet, not very thick; framed posters on the wall from the past, urging productivity and solidarity; chairs with arms and dark nylon padded seats and an old polished desk behind which, as on other occasions, sat Colonel Drozhkin.

Drozhkin looked even smaller this time than the last. His hair was just as white, his suit and tie just as black. The last time they had spoken, Drozhkin had indicated that he was, at the age of seventy-two, about to retire, but that clearly had not yet come to pass.

"Do you know why you are here?" Drozhkin said.

Rostnikov assumed that the question was somewhat rhetorical and shrugged, and then he observed from Drozhkin's face that the colonel did not know why the chief inspector was there.

"Do you know who wants to meet you?" Drozhkin said.

"No," said Rostnikov.

"General Shakhtyor, the miner," said Drozhkin, rising to glare angrily at Rostnikov. "Do you know who that is?"

"The name is familiar," said Rostnikov, watching the clearly frightened face of the old man before him.

"General Shakhtyor prefers it that way, prefers to be only vaguely known," said Drozhkin, coming out from behind his desk and approaching Rostnikov. Rostnikov was not a tall man, but Drozhkin stood several inches below him, and their eyes did not meet as the colonel stepped in front of him.

"The general is responsible for the Fifth Directorate," said Drozhkin. "Do you know what that is? You are a great policeman. Come, do you know what that is?"

"The Fifth Chief Directorate was created by the Politburo in 1969," said Rostnikov.

"For what purpose?" prodded Drozhkin like a schoolteacher grilling a slow student who has not done his homework.

"To deal with political problems," he said.

"To deal with—to remove—political dissent and to institute necessary control of the Soviet people who are politically suspect. Including intellectuals, Jews, religious sects, foreigners visiting the Soviet Union. You know this, Rostnikov."

"I've heard it, comrade colonel."

"When you attempted to blackmail the KGB into letting you emigrate to the United States, I had to deal with the issue through the Fifth Directorate. And now General Shakhtyor wants to see you. I would not trade the twenty years' difference in our ages to be in your position, Rostnikov."

"I am relieved," said Rostnikov. "I understand the Fifth Directorate is also interested in thought control and might actually have developed a way of exchanging old bodies for new, as they change old thoughts for new."

"You are a fool, Rostnikov, a fool," Drozhkin hissed, his pale face reddening.

And you, thought Rostnikov, *are very frightened*.

"Come on," said Drozhkin, grabbing the solid policeman's arm. Rostnikov let himself be turned and followed Drozhkin out of the room and down the green corridor, up a flight of stairs and deeper into the building. Drozhkin walked slowly, and Rostnikov had no difficulty keeping up with him. They said nothing to each other as they passed closed office doors. At the end of a corridor, Drozhkin stopped before a wooden door that was darker than others they had passed. He did not knock but stepped in, with Rostnikov behind him.

They were standing in a small office, which was carpeted. It seemed as if they had stepped into another world. It looked like the doctor's reception room he had once seen in an American magazine. There was a small painting of a seascape on the wall and a new desk behind which sat a rather pretty woman in glasses wearing a brown uniform. There were three waiting chairs, covered with black leather, across from the secretary. The woman stopped her work and looked up at the clock on the wall, indicating that they were perhaps a minute or two late.

"The general is expecting us," said Drozhkin, reaching up to touch his tie.

"The chief inspector is to go right in," she said.

Drozhkin walked past her desk, heading for the door behind her.

"The chief inspector is to go in alone," she said. Drozhkin stopped, hand still out, reaching toward the door.

Rostnikov glanced over at the seascape, and Drozhkin withdrew his hand and turned. From the corner of his eye. Rostnikov could see the old man's mouth tighten. Drozhkin, however, had fifty years of experience in both intimidation and humiliation, terror and compromise. He moved smoothly past Rostnikov and out the door.

"Knock" the secretary said, unsmiling. Rostnikov moved forward, recognizing that the brown carpet under his feet was appreciably thicker than that in Colonel Drozhkin's office.

He knocked and a deep voice answered, "Come in."

The office was at least twice the size of Drozhkin's, though the furniture was quite similar. There was a combination safe in the corner and a large window covered with a heavy screen. The window was open, and Rostnikov could see the courtyard beyond it. All this he took in without thought. His thoughts were concentrated on the man before him. The general had his back to Rostnikov and was doing something to a glass box atop the safe. The glass box, Rostnikov could see, was covered by a metal screen.

"Chameleons," the man said. "Do you want to take a look?"

The man's head was turned from him. It was bald and tight over his skull. He was slightly taller than Rostnikov and wearing a freshly pressed uniform of brown. Rostnikov moved to the man's side and looked into the aquarium. At first he could see nothing but a small cup of water and some rocks and twigs. And then one brown thickness on a twig twitched, and Rostnikov could see the chameleon blink its eyes. In a corner under the dish he then spotted the second chameleon, a bright green.

"They should be agents," the general said, still looking down at the creatures, which were no more than five inches long. "They blend into the background, can remain immobile for hours watching a moth or cricket before they move on it, and they are very durable. I've seen a moth die of fear after hours of being watched by a chameleon. Then, ironically, the chameleon refuses to eat it. They eat only living creatures."

And then, reluctantly, General Shakhtyor turned to his guest. They were about two feet apart when their eyes met. Rostnikov tried his best not to let his recognition show, but the old bald man, who looked like a bird of prey, probed his eyes, saw the recognition, nodded to himself, and stepped away.

"You want to sit?" he said, moving to a leather chair in front of the desk. There was a small table near the chair and another duplicate chair opposite the first. Rostnikov sat.

"Tea?" asked the general, his ancient eyes never leaving Rostnikov's face. The tea sat on the small table in a very decadent-looking porcelain samovar. There were two matching cups.

"Yes, thank you," said Rostnikov, sitting.

The general poured two cups with a steady hand and passed one to Rostnikov, who enjoyed the sudden heat on his palm.

"If your leg begins to hurt," said the general, "feel free to rise and move."

"Thank you," said Rostnikov.

"They like crickets and moths best," said Shakhtyor. "The chameleons. It is easy enough to get them in the summer, now, but in the winter they have to be obtained from our laboratory. Who knows why our laboratory breeds insects?"

He drank, the brown eyes in his tight face always on Rostnikov. Their shrewdness tested Rostnikov, but he controlled himself.

"I have two stories for you, chief inspector," he said. "When I am through, you are to choose one."

"Comrade—" Rostnikov began.

The general held up a bony hand and stopped him. "Indulge me," he said. "I'm a very old man."

Rostnikov sat back, holding his tea in two hands.

"A man named Shmuel Prensky left the village of Yekteraslav almost sixty years ago," said the general, watching Rostnikov's eyes. "He was a promising young Jew, but by then, it was becoming quite evident that there would be no place for Jews in the Soviet system, at least no place of real power. Trotsky's expulsion had settled that. Shmuel Prensky died. I knew him. I was at his side when it happened. It was during an attempt to quell an agricultural uprising not far from Tbilisi. So, he died."

The old man looked at Rostnikov, who nodded to show that he was listening and understood.

"Then," the general went on, "many years later, some

friends of Prensky's youth, who were old men, began to settle ancient scores. A lout named Mikhail Posniky, seeking revenge, came from America and killed one of the other old friends, Abraham Savitskaya. I don't know the circumstances."

"He was reading *Izvestia* in the bathtub when he was shot," said Rostnikov.

The old man narrowed his eyes to determine if Rostnikov was risking levity, but he could not detect it with certainty. So he went on.

"And during the subsequent investigation," he said, "the name of the now-dead Shmuel Prensky came up. Then there was good luck followed by bad. You found this killer, this Mikhail Posniky. That was good. Unfortunately, the killer was run down by a hit-and-run driver. Case closed. A fine job done by the police. But you did not close the investigation. You went to a retired assistant procurator and got her to delve into the old files on this Prensky."

"It was another case, another old man," Rostnikov said, finishing his tea. "A man named Lev Ostrovsky who worked in the Moscow Art Theatre, a man who mentioned the name Shmuel Prensky before he died. It was that murder I was investigating."

"I admire your dedication to justice," said the old general, putting his hand to his shaved head. "Even after you were told to forget, to stay out of the files."

Rostnikov shrugged.

"How much do you understand here, chief inspector?"

"Too much," Rostnikov sighed.

"Too much," the general agreed. "Now for the other story."

"I'm not sure I have to hear it," said Rostnikov softly.

"It's too late," said Shakhtyor, leaning back. "This is a fairy-tale alternative. What if Shmuel Prensky did not die, huh? What if another young revolutionary died and this Shmuel Prensky simply took his place? It could happen. It happened all the time. Shmuel Prensky, the Jew from Yekteraslav, becomes a Gentile orphan and demonstrates his value to the state with years of devotion."

"Like a chameleon," said Rostnikov.

"Somewhat," agreed the general, "but the analogy is limited. The environment of the chameleon is minimal and simple. Human life is not so simple. I'll go on with my story. Prensky, who is now living a new life, moves up in the military, eventually goes into intelligence work, and rises high in the KGB. It could happen."

"It could happen," agreed Rostnikov, shifting his leg.

"More tea?" asked the general, and Rostnikov agreed. "But the new life did not exist without shreds of the old. Two old friends from Yekteraslav, old friends who had once taken a photograph together, know about the new life, but the former Shmuel Prensky is not without loyalty to his past life. He finds work for them, a job for the one called Abraham, who has come back from the United States, come back to escape the vengeance of the other old friend he betrayed. And then there is the actor, the fool. They serve a purpose, have a function, to keep the barrier between the past and present covered. You see where we are going, Rostnikov?"

Rostnikov nodded that he understood, and something like a grin appeared on the ancient beak before him.

"Shmuel Prensky could have had the old friends killed, but they were old friends, and they cost little," the general went on. "They served as extra ears. But when this Mikhail Posniky came back, this gangster from America, things changed. Prensky's name began to draw attention. You began to draw attention to it. So what could Prensky do? Had Mikhail Posniky gotten on his plane and left, all would have been fine, but he did not. You were too efficient."

"Thank you," said Rostnikov dryly.

"And so Shmuel Prensky had the gangster from America killed. And knowing that the chief inspector would go back to the actor, he managed just in time to have someone beat him to the theater and dispose of the old man. And so . . ."

"Only Shmuel Prensky remains," finished Rostnikov. "The fourth man in the photograph."

"If you prefer the second tale," agreed the general. "Which do you prefer?"

"The first," said Rostnikov, putting down his cup. He had drunk enough tea. His stomach felt uneasy. In the corner the chameleons scurried over rocks, rustling the cage.

"Then Shmuel Prensky is dead," said the general with a smile.

"Dead," agreed Rostnikov.

"Would you like to continue living?" the general said matter-of-factly, pressing his hands together.

"I would prefer it to the alternative," Rostnikov said, controlling his voice and quite aware that the old man was watching the inspector's hands to see if there might be a betraying tremor.

"Good," said the old man. "If you were to die, there are so many people who have heard of the name of Shmuel Prensky—the assistant procurator; Anna Timofeyeva, the former assistant procurator; your two or three assistants; perhaps your wife. You could all have accidents, but that might draw attention to this situation, might make others who have ears in the KGB suspicious, might get them asking questions. No, if you live and let the matter drop, see to it that the matter drops, questions about Shmuel Prensky end. Of course you can be, will continue to be, watched, listened to, checked. A mind can always change. Six or seven accidents can always be arranged. It would be simple to do so. You understand?"

"Fully," said Rostnikov.

"One more thing," said the old man, rising. "Colonel Drozhkin does not know about this Shmuel Prensky fairy tale. Very few people have heard the story. Colonel Drozhkin also believes that you have dangerous information secreted outside of the country, information that would provide evidence that the KGB arranged for the murder of a dissident several years ago."

"Yes," said Rostnikov, also rising.

"That evidence is worthless," said the general, moving back to the chameleons on his safe. "If it were released now, we would simply deny it or suggest that it was the plan of Yuri Andropov when he was responsible here. In a world where people are obsessed with oil and bombs, your information would be lost. I do not, however, plan to share this observation with Colonel Drozhkin. He might well decide to remove you and possibly your charming Jewish wife and your son, the soldier."

"I understand," Rostnikov said, keeping himself from clenching his fists.

"Good," said the general. "You are a good policeman. I've examined your file. Go back to being a policeman. You might yet have a long life."

It might have been a dismissal, but Rostnikov stood while the old bird tapped at the wire mesh atop the cage to get the attention of the chameleons.

"You have a question, chief inspector?" he said without turning.

"In your fairy tale, general, Shmuel Prensky betrays his own people, becomes the claw that grips the Jews?"

The general stopped tapping and turning to look at Rostnikov. Rostnikov had gone too far. He knew it, knew he should have simply left, but it had come almost unbidden. It had come as a small sign of his own remaining dignity.

"Shmuel Prensky in the tale survives," the general said. "He survives and prospers. He knows that distinctions such as Jew, Christian, capitalist, Greek, are meaningless, that they stand in the way of progress, that they are artificial barriers created by petty humans to preserve minimal distinctions that evade and avoid progress. Shmuel Prensky in the tale knows that people are and must be equal, that differences based on myths must be eliminated. Shmuel Prensky in the tale lives for progress."

"But Shmuel Prensky is dead," said Rostnikov.

"Quite dead," said the general. "Now leave and tell no fairy tales. Leave before I decide that your final moment of audacity is simple stupidity."

Rostnikov went to the door, feeling the old eyes on him, went out and walked past the secretary, who did not look up. Outside, in the green corridor, Drozhkin stood waiting.

"What did he say? What did he want?" the colonel said.

"It had nothing to do with you," said Rostnikov, moving forward in the general direction of the stairway. "I'm permitted to say no more."

Drozhkin's teeth came together tightly, and he strode in front of Rostnikov, led the way out of the Center, and stepped back at the front lobby without letting his eyes meet the detective's.

Rostnikov, in turn, did not glance back but crossed the lobby as a quartet of men flowed around him. He went out the door and into the square where he continued to control himself. He wanted to let himself shake, wanted some slackness to ease the mask into which he had set his face, but he dared not, feared he was being watched.

His mind insisted on the fleeting thought that the Soviet nation was run by ancient men like the colonel, the general, by the Chernenkos. That the old eventually died and the young became the old. Only when he had gone down the stairs of the Dzerzhinsky metro station across the square on Kirov Street did he allow his facial muscles to loosen a bit, his shoulders to drop slightly. He had survived, was alive, had not been ushered into the depths of Lubyanka. He was alive and would have dinner that evening, if a hit-and-run driver did not appear, with his wife and son.

Rostnikov would worry about tomorrow, tomorrow. In Moscow that was the only way it could be.

EPILOGUE

THE WORLD CHANGED RAPIDLY FOR PORFIRY PETROvich Rostnikov that morning. When he returned to his office, he discovered that Assistant Procurator Khabolov no longer wanted to see him. In fact, the central operator made it quite clear that Assistant Procurator Khabolov did not want to see him ever again for any reason. It was Zelach who told Rostnikov the rumor that Khabolov was packing his things, that he was being transferred. The rumor was that he was going back to his former service as a security officer, but this time at a telephone factory near Leningrad.

In the course of that hour, after discovering that he was going to live at least for a while, Rostnikov further discovered that:

—Emil Karpo was going to have the surgery and that Sarah's cousin Alex would do it in his office.

—That the car thief named Marina would not have a public trial and, therefore, Tkach's indiscretion would not be part of the record.

—That Anna Timofeyeva was in Petrovka and headed for the file room.

Rostnikov intercepted Anna on the stairway and led her to his office where he explained that the pursuit of the old man named Shmuel Prensky was over, that Shmuel Prensky was dead. Something in her shrewd eyes made it clear that she recognized that more existed to the tale, but she accepted it with a nod, shared tea with Rostnikov, and excused herself after saying, "Were you a fool again, Porfiry Petrovich?"

"I was a fool," he said, sighing. "But I survive. A very important man told me today that survival is the most important thing there is. What do you think?"

"Survival isn't enough," she said. "There has to be meaning with it or we are just animals."

When she had gone, Rostnikov examined his few case files, all minor cases. He ran his finger along the scratch on his desk, took the object from his desk that he had placed there the night before, and left Petrovka, telling the scowling Zelach to take messages.

A half hour later he knocked at the door to the apartment of Sofiya Savitskaya. She opened it, and he could see that she was once again alone. He handed her the candlestick.

"The man who killed your father is dead," he said. "He confessed and then was accidentally run over. He was an old enemy, half mad. It had something to do with a childhood disagreement back in the village where they were born."

He didn't step into the small apartment, though he could smell some sweet food being cooked within. The woman clutched the candlestick, and Rostnikov reached into his pocket for an envelope.

"The photograph," he said, handing this to her. "All of the men in the picture are dead."

He waited for her to say something, but no words came from her. She looked at him as if she were still waiting for him to speak, as if he had been silent. He wondered how much she had understood and how mad all of this had made her. He hoped that the candlestick would once again be dormant in her humid little apartment. Before she could close the door, he turned and went down the hall.

When he got back to his apartment, neither Sarah nor Josef was there, but the phone was ringing. At first he considered letting it ring, ignoring it, but he knew he could not.

"Rostnikov," he grunted.

"This is Major Malekov of the militia," came the flat voice. "I am to inform you that as of tomorrow you are to take up duties on the investigative staff of Colonel Snitkonoy on special assignment."

"I assume, then, that you have just so informed me," said Rostnikov. "Unless you wish to repeat what you have just said."

"I simply want your acknowledgment, Comrade Rostnikov," the major said.

"You have it, major," he said, and hung up the phone.

And so, he thought, *I am to be exiled to the Gray Wolfhound*. It could be worse, much worse, but it could also be much better. He made himself an American-style sandwich with canned mackerel and read two chapters from the McBain book he had been savoring. Carella was puzzled by an ax murderer, but he would find him. Isola would be saved again. It was reassuring.

It was some time before six when the key turned in the door. Rostnikov rose, wiped his mouth with his sleeve, and watched the door open. Josef, light, handsome, uniformed, looked over at his father and smiled, and Rostnikov smiled back, limping forward to give the young man a massive bear hug of love.

ABOUT THE AUTHOR

Stuart M. Kaminsky is the author of five Inspector Rostnikov mysteries: DEATH OF A DISSIDENT, BLACK KNIGHT IN RED SQUARE (an Edgar nominee), RED CHAMELEON, A FINE RED RAIN and A COLD RED SUNRISE. He now teaches film history, criticism and production at Northwestern University, where he is a professor and head of the Division of Film. He lives in Skokie, Illinois, with his wife and three children.